COVID-NINETEEN LIVES

Lisa J Rivers

GREEN CAT BOOKS

Published in 2020

by GREEN CAT BOOKS
19 St Christopher's Way
Pride Park
Derby
DE24 8JY
www.green-cat.co

Cover art by Carisse Rivers

CONTENTS

We Have the Technology

The board room was fully attended by the scheduled meeting time of 9 a.m.

"Happy New Year, everyone," the PM addressed his team.

There were a few grunts around the table.

"Happy new century!" Edward, Minister of Defence replied.

"Yes indeed," the PM responded. "Ok, so I hope you all had a great break. Now, the turn of the new century brings with it the hope of better technology. I am meeting at the UN very soon and wish to discuss the subject with other leaders while I'm there. Who of you are technologically minded enough to put forward some ideas of how we can move our country, and the world forward?"

"'Ow about sorting out some way to pay at the checkouts without 'avin' to deal with a human?" Beryl, the tea lady laughed as she dished out the refreshments.

"Well, yes, actually that isn't a bad idea," PM Grant agreed. "The queues do drive me mad too, Mrs Baxter!"

Beryl chuckled as she added plates of pastries to the table.

"Thank you, Mrs Baxter," he concluded, as she exited with her rattly trolley.

"Michelle, as Minister of Technology, could this be a possibility?"

"Erm, yes, Prime Minister. Not wanting to state the obvious, but computer technology has advanced greatly over the past few decades. Back then, the only way something feasible like this would be achieved by creating human-like robots to sit in seats and act in the same way as a sales assistant would. But now we can do so much more."

"But wouldn't this increase unemployment to an unprecedented number?" Mike, Minister of Employment questioned.

"Yes," Michelle confirmed, "it's an issue, of course. Staff would still be needed to help out customers who struggle with technology."

"Security officers would also still be needed. No robots could ever be competent enough to spot a thief, unless machines were brought in to scan every customer as they enter and exit a store," Edward added.

"That would slow customers down even more than keeping people on the checkouts," Mike responded.

"So we need to decide which is more important; a technically-advanced nation which leans towards the consumer, or staying in the twentieth century to keep unemployment rates down?" Prime Minister Grant questioned.

"With the rise in technology, more people would be employed to create these products, to programme them..." Michelle explained.

"Yes," Mike replied, "but the people currently employed as checkout staff, our nation's blue-collar workers in general won't have the ability to adapt into such a role, it would take longer to train them than keeping them on the checkouts."

"So we need to slowly introduce the new checkout technology, keeping regular checkouts open too, for both the consumers and the employees to adapt to, plus providing an option depending on ability and preference."

A few mutters echoed round the room. They stopped for a break to mull things over, drinking tepid drinks poured out of thermal tea and coffee pots and devouring the pastries. Mrs Baxter returned to collect the empty crockery and replaced the drinks vessels with fresh ones.

Everyone reconvened and the topic was set to continue.

"Ok, my esteemed colleagues, now that we have exhausted Mrs Baxter's suggestion, do we have any more ideas to advance our country technologically!" Grant restarted the proceedings.

"What direction are you wanting the technology to go in, Prime Minister?"

"Well, let's continue with ways to speed up the checkout for now," he suggested, a couple of the ministers groaning. "Before you all start grumbling, do you remember when debit cards were introduced? How much simpler, and quicker are they than when we used to write cheques? The cashier just swipes it into the machine, you sign a receipt and hey presto!"

"My mother still insists on going into a bank to draw out money, rather than working out how to use ATM machines, let alone paying by card in a shop!" Geoff, Minister for Agriculture stated.

"Well, it's up to the younger community to help bring their relatives into this new, advanced 21st century!" Grant responded.

"Sir," a young woman stood up.

"Yes, Natalie?" Grant replied.

"As Secretary of State for Environment, can we find a way to reduce waste in these large supermarkets, sir?"

"Yes, that was one of the issues raised recently too. In what ways do you suggest, Natalie."

"Well, the eradication of cheques completely, for a start. This would reduce the use of paper, which benefits the environment, plus it will reduce debt in this country at the same time." She gestured to the minister for finance. "The numbers, I believe, are high for debt, as users can pay with cheques and cheque guarantee cards when they may have insufficient funds in their banks to cover it. I appreciate that this could affect the hardship of such people who do this despite the knowledge that they will receive bank charges."

Finance Minister Llewellyn nodded. "I agree with my esteemed colleague, debt caused this way does need to improve."

"And maybe something as simple as an extra receipt to sign for the payment could be eradicated?" Minister Natalie added.

"What do you think, technologically, Michelle?"

The minister considered this for a moment, her brow furrowing. "How about an ID card? I'm thinking this may only be possible in the more distant future, as it would entail stricter citizen control, I would imagine.

"Like a passport, but as a card instead. Similar to a driving licence card. All info, such as bank balances, date of birth, travel rights instead of a separate passport, and so on."

"Well, that sounds great, but also could create uproar amongst society who consider this a way of control, 'Big brother'; an infringement on their basic human rights."

"Thank you, Craig. Human rights are a big issue. Introducing a national ID card would be beneficial for many, for such issues as crime, for example, especially to check a criminal record. It would avoid giving false names, it could track the whereabouts of suspects to avoid false alibis. It could provide better security for border controls. But yes, this does seem to be a long way off right now."

The prime minister allowed a small recess while he mulled this idea over some more. Cups chinked together and Mrs Baxter appeared with platters of sandwiches, cakes and fruit. She returned an hour later to clean the luncheon area and provided more pots of hot drinks.

Order was called, everyone returned to their seats.

"Ok, back to technological advances," Prime Minister Grant announced. "From what I can think, the ID card can be feasible in the near future, but not immediately. If I remember correctly, there has been some unrest about parts of the UK wanting to leave the European Union, is that right, Secretary Esmail?"

"Thank you, Prime Minister, yes, there is talk of this. There is a small minority that are supporters of the UKIP party, sir, who want just that. It is unlikely to become significant though."

"Well maybe that's something to consider as a step forward for more stringent border controls. Not necessarily to restrict entry into the UK for immigrants, which I believe is one of UKIPs main goals, but rather to introduce new passports, or indeed these ID Cards."

Silence fell amongst the ministers as they considered this.

"In conclusion then, we do need to discuss eliminating the ability to purchase items using cheques with their promissory cards, and taking steps to improve debit cards to reduce paper wastage, for the purpose of a leap forward for ecology and the eradication of debt," Prime Minister Grant summarised. "Is there a possibility that, perhaps, a very small microchip could be added to any type of transactional card to store and share information, Michelle?"

"There is no doubt, Mr Prime Minister, that it is possible. It would mean a huge overhaul throughout the UK to upgrade their machinery to an acceptable level. It would take time, and money, but is attainable."

"In the interim, sir," the foreign minister suggested, "as a step towards the ID cards, we could introduce small microchips to passports. Adding this as an upgrade when citizens renew their documents would be a gentle introduction without too much fuss."

"Yes, that could work," Grant agreed. "It will all take a

while to implement, but it all sounds reasonable. The long-term goal is to make all consumer related transactions contactless in the future."

"What do you mean 'contactless', sir?" Edward enquired.

The prime minister gestured to the finance minister.

"Well, on the internet currently there are websites which sell items, and payments are collected by independent payment companies. For example, eBay allows the general public to sell items, securely collect payments by another company called PayPal, and the seller and buyer can literally be anywhere in the world that the item can be posted to, with no handing over cash or signing payment slips, or indeed face-to-face transactions."

Grant interceded, "Heaven forbid we have a health crisis like, say the flu epidemic less than a century ago. Over 500 million were infected worldwide, and killed around ten percent of that, and it was spread through contact. If that were to happen a hundred years later," he rustled some papers, "that was 1918, so in 2018, just 17 years from now, with an even larger world population, the results could be catastrophic. If contactless resources were available as standard, there would be less casualties, and the population would be familiarised with the system ahead of time, causing minimal chaos."

The meeting room telephone interrupted the discussion. Grant answered it.

"Ok ladies and gentlemen, that concludes the meeting for today. We will convene again before my visit to the UN, let's put our thinking caps on and find solutions before the problems arise, Let's be proactive!"

We Have the Control

"Statistics show that Earth is rapidly dying, due to the humans taking what they believe is theirs, and not facing the consequences," Milo reported to his immediate supervisor, Judy.

"OK, let's look at the facts that we have, the history of the planet," Judy replied, with concern in her voice.

She tapped on several glass screens at head height, around four feet from the ground, suspended simply, with forced gravity designed specifically for this room. Moving a selection of sub-screens out of the way, she found the correct file; 'Earth Interventions'.

"I can see that we have interfered with the preservation of the inhabitants of Earth quite a few times. However, all of the other times it has been due to natural disasters. Meteors, floods, earthquakes, tsunamis...." Judy continued to swipe through the files. "Such activities have caused controversy amongst our people. Senior advisors claim that natural disasters strike for a reason and should be left well alone. They say that extinctions of species must continue otherwise the natural order of the universe will be affected.

"The majority of the inhabitants apparently believe that there's an invisible magic person who lives in the sky. They say that 'He', with a capital 'H', controls all of the disasters, but in the same breath say that 'He' will also protect them. It makes no sense to me at all." They both laughed and Milo shook his head.

"Well, they are half right, there are magic 'people' who live in the sky," he joked.

"Humans, although fairly advanced, would still go into a mass hysteria if they all knew about us. Yet a 'God', with a capital 'G', can not only love them unconditionally, but can cause natural disasters that kill hundreds of thousands. And then..." Judy continued, struggling to keep her composure, "they 'pray', which basically is a magic plea where they close their eyes and hands, for a 'miracle', asking this 'God' to heal people who have been afflicted by the disasters that 'He' caused."

"Yes, agreed Milo, "I don't think are quite at the right intellectual level just yet!" They both laughed hysterically.

"if only they knew all of it, eh Milo?!" Judy stated, and they laughed some more. "Ok, ok, let's get back to the matter in hand now. Sara?"

"Yes, Judy?" a slight female approached them both.

"Can you check what methods we have used in the past to control the human population increase, please?"

"Sure can, boss, just give me a few seconds." Sara tapped away at her screen. "Plagues, boss."

"Plagues?" Judy repeated. "How effective have they been, Sara?"

"Millions, boss," Sara explained. "In some cases, 30 plus million."

"Ah, excellent, Sara. I doubt we'd need that many, and it would need to target the rich as well as the poor, which I believe were the usual victims, if memory serves."

"Yes, Judy," the historian responded, "you are quite right, it was the poor."

"It was usually spread by rats though, ladies," Milo interrupted.

"OK, there are still rats though, aren't there, Milo?" Judy questioned.

"Yes, ma'am, but they usually stick to the poorer areas, so wouldn't really target the rich."

"Ah, well we really need to aim for the wealthier humans, they are the ones who are destroying rain forests," Zach, Earth Environmental Officer stated, as he approached the small team. "They hunt animals just for sport, for trophies, and these are partly the reason why so many endangered species are becoming extinct. It wasn't a big deal when it was the dodo, as they were stupid creatures, but breeds of wild cats, rhinos..." he looked at the others, who had questioning expressions on their faces, "well, all kinds of animals are becoming extinct unnecessarily. It's not through natural selection, it is pure, cruel slaughter."

"Cats!" Kent blurted out.

No-one had even known he was in the room. "Whoa there, Kent! We all know that you like animals too," Judy mocked the young animal enthusiast, who was still in learning mode.

"No, I mean there are a lot more cats on Earth nowadays, whereas back in the days of plagues, they weren't around to catch and kill the rats. I believe that, I think it was the black plague several hundred Earth years ago, deaths were a lot lower than further back in history, and it was because the cats killed the rats, who were spreading the disease."

"Good job, Kent," Judy exclaimed with pride. "You have done well, I'm recommending you for a merit award. Could you do a full assignment for me, please, on the plagues of Earth, outlining how they started, spread and where please. And of course, how they were eradicated?"

"Oh, yes Ma'am. I shall do that right away."

"Great, let's see if we can get you a distinction!" Judy said proudly, as he whizzed off to his workstation.

She turned back to the other crew. "We'll need to set up a meeting with all the leaders. Sara, can you get the chap from Earth Leader Liaisons, erm...,"

"Knox, ma'am," Sara assisted.

"Yes, thanks, ask Knox to arrange it, please."

Sara nipped over to her workstation to send a message.

"I'm just waiting for them all to respond, Sara," Knox replied almost immediately.

She relayed this to her superior, Judy.

"Bloody humans are so slow!" the impatient leader complained. "Ok, let's get some work done, ready for when they are."

Judy was used to getting things done in a flash, not in the Earth days like the UN completed jobs. Plus they had something that they liked to call a 'weekend', which meant that some had 2 Earth days when they wouldn't work at all, except for heating up foods and maintaining their natural assigned areas.

"China, ma'am," Kent appeared out of nowhere.

"Oh, Kent, you made me jump!"

"Sorry, ma'am. China appears to be the best place to start a plague. It has the largest population, from what I can see, and they don't have cats. Well, not as pets or stray animals, they are more like … a delicacy."

"I see. Well, that's great, Kent, well done. What else can you tell me?"

"We could try a modern-day virus, ma'am," Sara interjected. "Something, hmmm... manufactured."

"Oooh, interesting," said Kent, tapping on his handheld device. "If it is more modern, it'll be more sophisticated. That means it will take them longer to figure it out."

"I think even the leaders of Earth will not be able to figure it out," Judy pondered. "Do you think we should cut out the middleman and just go for it?"

The team nodded.

"To be fair, ma'am," Knox added, "even those who are advanced still won't know what to do. They are so much slower than us, and they will be slower than the virus too."

Judy mulled it over a little. "Maybe it will actually unify countries that have been at war. They may actually learn something from this lesson, and it could bring peace to them all, create a new kind of intelligent human and allow us to eventually settle after all."

"One or two leaders may react quickly and combat it in no time. These will be the more advanced inhabitants," Knox commented.

"Right then, let's get this plan into action. To start in China, Kent?"

Here's to a New Year

"Next year is going to be so much better than this year has been," Donna stated, to no-one in particular.

She had organised a small party, as she did every year. The texts had been sent, food had been bought, and alcohol of all descriptions; spirits, beers, wines, and even a couple of bottles of champagne for midnight were on display on her breakfast bar.

Her little council flat was heaving with inebriated twenty-somethings last year, and she expected the same again tonight. She gave the whole place a massive clean and then set about preparing the little 'horse derves', as she put it. Chicken goujons, sausage rolls, garlic bread, mozzarella bites, pigs in blankets, sausage rolls and Indian snacks like onion bhajis and samosas. She hadn't forgotten the sweet treats either; mince pies, Christmas cake and stollen, 'croaky bush', chocolate Yule log, and 'chocolatey claires'.

She had invited and catered for about 60 to the party, including all of her mates down at the office where she worked. They'd had a right mash up at the office party a couple of weeks ago, when they went to 'Harveys' for an all-inclusive meal and entertainment package, where dancing on the tables was not only expected, but encouraged. That was where she had met her boyfriend, Albie, who was dancing in the hallway that led to the toilets. They'd literally bumped into each other and hit it off straight away. They had both danced on their own table for the rest of the night, downing complimentary multicoloured shots out of test tubes until they threw up!

Since then, they had been inseparable, except for Christmas day, of course, which he spent with his parents, and she spent with her family. For the rest of the week, they had eaten to breaking point, and drank until they could drink no more.

Albie had stayed over at Donna's flat since Boxing Day and emerged from the bathroom in his party regalia, offering to help out with the catering. Donna took control of the cooked items, as that was her domain, so he was left with emptying boxes and putting items neatly on plates. They assembled the croquembouche together, falling about in a semi-drunken stupor halfway through.

"It can be a 'croaky sit down' instead, lol," Albie laughed, struggling to stick the profiteroles with the toffee.

"Why would they even call it a bush though," Donna replied, "it doesn't even look like a bush!"

"Maybe it's meant to be 'crooked' rather than 'croaky," he suggested, lifting Donna up and carrying her into the bedroom.

They were just returning from the bedroom when the first of the visitors arrived.

"I'm not even ready yet!" Donna exclaimed.

"You look hot to me!" Albie smirked. "Go and get ready and I'll see to the guests."

She blew him a kiss and disappeared back into the bedroom.

"Hiyyeeee...." the guests shouted, before checking the door number, worried that they had the wrong flat.

"Hi. I'm Albie," he introduced himself, smiling and letting them in.

Six young girls stumbled in, already half cut.

"That's Kelly, Bex, Ange, Lettie, Shay and I'm Jools," the young blonde announced. "Where's Don?"

"She's just in the bedroom getting ready," Albie replied.

"Yeah, sounds like 'er!" Kelly laughed, and they all cackled in agreement.

"I remember you," Lettie announced, "You were there at Harveys last week."

"Yep," Albie replied, smiling. "Help yourself to food and drink."

Bottles clinked as they relieved their carrier bags of a selection of wines. One rummaged in a kitchen drawer and found the corkscrew, while another fished some wine glasses out of the cupboard. They were busy with the booze and snacks when Donna emerged from the bedroom, fully made up and in a slinky purple dress.

"Ooooooh!" the girls chorused.

"I see the theme is purple this year, Don!" Bex announced.

"Yep!" Donna replied. "There were tons of balloons to blow up, but we never had time." She flushed a bit, remembering how they had spent the last few days.

"Well, let's get doing it now then!"

They all sat round the helium machine that was in the corner of the living area and in no time they were all inflated and dancing on the ceiling. Of course, there was some helium left over, so they all revelled in high-pitched voices. Albie topped all of their glasses up and Donna switched on her Bluetooth and connected her smart phone to her soundbar.

"Woooo, tunes of the…… What would the last decade be called? The first 9 years of the 2000s were the noughties, so… teens?"

"Sounds a bit suspect to me, babe!" Kelly replied.

The door knocked again. Screeches indicated that it was more intoxicated girls. Donna invited them in and introduced them to her work mates and Albie.

"These are my mates from school," she explained, naming them all.

"You know I'm not going to remember any of these, dontcha?" Albie announced.

"Yeah, babe, it's all cool," Donna replied, kissing him.

"Break it up, will ya!" one of them interrupted them. "Some of us need drinks!"

"Awight, Els," Donna replied, staggering over to the breakfast bar that separated the kitchen area from the living area.

They had to start on the paper cups now, as all the wine glasses were in use. "I tried to get the plastic wine glasses, but they were all sold out, so I had to get these. They ain't even purple!"

Ellie tapped the red cup, "They're eco-friendly though!"

They cackled as Donna filled the cups.

Soon the flat was overwhelmed with people that Donna didn't directly know, but the vibe was good, and the drinks were plenty. There was barely enough room to dance, but they managed.

"Nothing wrong with a little bump 'n' grind!" Ellie said, as she started dancing with a fella from Donna's work.

"Just watch 'im," Donna replied, "He's a bit of a ladies' man, apparently."

Ellie smiled, and got even closer to him.

More and more people swamped the flat. Donna prepared more hors d'oeuvres and grabbed a bottle of rum out of her kitchen cupboard and prepared batches of mojitos.

"Mojes, anyone?" she announced as she poured enough for everyone. A load roar erupted amongst the group.

More people arrived and the flat was heaving with bodies. Shaun, the bloke from downstairs turned up. Donna thought he was there to complain about the noise.

"I'm sorry, mate, do you need us to turn it down a bit?" she asked, hoping he didn't.

"No, not at all!" he replied. "Thought I'd gatecrash!"

"Fabulous!" Donna replied, shoving a mojito into his hand.

He seemed to be older than everyone else there, but that didn't stop him from having a good time. He was dancing with some of the girls from work, who were swarming him.

Lettie turned the music up on Donna's phone and a few of them sang along, very out of tune and very loud.

"Lav it!" Donna shouted, to no-one in particular.

The alarm sounded on her phone, stunning everyone motionless, like a game of musical statues. Donna dashed over to the phone to cancel the alarm and switched off the playlist.

"Everyone, it's nearly midnight, and the church down the road is doing a midnight fireworks display. Some of us are gonna head down there, anyone who wants to come is welcome, or you are welcome to stay in the warmth of my flat," she laughed.

She went into her bedroom and started sorting through all of the coats that had been flung on her bed, handing them out to whoever needed one. Suitable wrapped, a few of them trekked along the street.

Reverent Fred and members of his congregation were handing out warm mulled wine to keep the crowds warm. Mrs Everly had some leftover mince pies too, and a couple of the newcomers accepted this token of friendship. Her son, Jacob was fussing over the fireworks, placing the last of them strategically. He paced impatiently, waiting for the nod from the reverend to light the first in the sequence. Donna and her posse moved closer to a bonfire that the church had built.

"Feels like Fireworks Day," Donna stated to Albie, who had his arms around his girlfriend to keep her warm.

He nodded and embraced her tighter. The reverend shouted to the crowd, who fell silent.

"It's just one minute until midnight, are we all ready for the countdown?"

The crowd cheered and started counting down. Jacob knew that this was the prompt to start the fireworks. At 'five', he lit the first firework, which zoomed into the air and showered sparkles of green over the onlookers.

"Woooo!" the crowd shouted and applauded.

This first firework set off a consecutive display of multicoloured illuminations, a couple redirecting to the next display, igniting a few out of sequence. Jacob was enraged, having spent hours arranging everything. The crowd ducked and dived to avoid uncontrollable rockets which were shooting in all directions. Jacob ran over to the unlit fireworks in a violent frenzy and kicked them, not realising that a rogue spark would set them off. The crowds dispersed, running for their lives, screaming and pushing.

Donna trotted along with Albie as best she could in the stilettos she was wearing, and spotted a couple getting a little too frisky amongst the graveyard headstones.

"That's just wrong, man! There are dead people there, they should be left to rest in pieces!" The woman looked up, it was Kelly. "Kels, you dirty bitch, you've got a boyfriend back at the flat!"

The man laughed, pulling Kelly back down. Donna stomped over to the couple, to give her a piece of her mind. The man was Shaun.

"SHAUN! You have a wife back at home, what are you playing at?"

"Get lost, you frigid little cow," Kelly screeched, pulling away from Shaun and heading for Donna.

Albie and Shaun managed to stop a confrontation between the two, as the reverend and his wife looked on in dismay.

"I'm so sorry, ref, I didn't know they were going to dessicate your beautiful home. They are disgusting." Donna was mortified and close to tears.

Albie comforted her on the way back to her flat. The warmth of her home was stifling, and the mix of cold, anger, mulled wine and the Irish cream drinks she had consumed earlier disagreed with Donna, and she dashed to her bathroom.

She spent the rest of the night sitting on the bathroom floor, sobbing at the various substances that had appeared on her bathroom carpet. Albie occasionally visited her with glasses of water, and to hold her hair and give her updates about the partygoers.

The last of the revellers remained when Donna finally surfaced. She stepped over slumped friends, and friends of friends and sat on her sofa, her nerves racked with emotion.

"I'm never having another new year party!" she

announced to Albie, who sat on the arm of the sofa next to her.

"Hey, nothing wrong with ending on a high, babe. Let's toast to a new decade," he suggested, holding up his mug of coffee.

Donna raised her glass of water and clinked it against Albie's drink.

"I fink 2020 is going to be our year, Alb," she replied.

Borderline

I usually don't wake up until around midday. My prescription medication knocks me out for around 12 to 14 hours a day, but without them I function even less. Sofa replaces my bed once up; my duvet is replaced by a fluffy blanket in the living room.

I carry my bottle containing tap water around with me, I'm usually unable to stand in the kitchen long enough to make a hot drink. Packets of readily available snacks sit beside my corner of the sofa.

Also by my side is a notebook and pen, for when inspiration comes to me and I need to write; whether it is a poem or story. There is a laptop that I can use, if my strength allows.

I like to keep my brain active – it is the only asset I have left.

Simple activities like colouring books with pens every colour of the rainbow, and more, keep me distracted when my eyes focus enough. Sometimes I colour outside of the lines, but I don't care. I am under no illusion, I know I am no artist. The colours, and the flowing motion sooth me; distract me from my aches and pains.

Assuming that my migraines are under control, I find yellow to be my energising colour. On low pain days, I have managed to adapt my two living spaces with as much cheerful décor as possible. Oil burners emanate the sweet smells of citrus from my essential oils. When my migraines attack, I simply choose a different selection of aromas to sooth.

I used to knit, but my hands hurt too much now. A strange numbness would appear, indicating poor circulation, but this didn't make sense. The more I moved my fingers, the heavier they felt.

$\mathbf{M}$y slow decline in health had been difficult to spot when my children were younger, but looking back, there was a huge difference. At one time, I had been able to cook for my children, drive them to school, take them to the park. Now they had grown up and left home, my duties had dwindled, and I served no purpose anymore.

I could have chosen to stay in bed all the time, to nap when my body demanded, but I refuse to let this debilitating illness take over my life completely.

$\mathbf{M}$y husband is my rock. He works 2 jobs to support us both, and still manages to fetch my prescriptions, ensure that there is a meal available whenever we need to eat, and help me wash and dress.

$\mathbf{D}$uring the COVID pandemic he still worked his 2 jobs, but fortunately his shift times changed. Hospitals needed him more to deliver prescriptions at silly times, usually overnight, but he was allowed a few hours off during the day, so he started coming home in the day, around the time I got up.

It was lovely to have him around. We had lunch together every day. Even though he was home less than before, I got to spend more time with him as at least I was awake when he was here. Those couple of hours a day were the best we'd had for years. Working two jobs had taken its toll on him. The strain was visible to me; just because I was ill, didn't mean I was stupid.

He refused to believe that I was ill, of course, just couldn't accept that his wife was slowly fading away. Money was tight for us as I could no longer work, which was why he works two jobs.

My carer told me that we could claim benefits to make money a bit easier, and even offered to help me, but Tom is a proud man, didn't like to take charity. Instead, he dutifully worked these two jobs and paid for everything, from my prescriptions to the care company he hired to provide the extra help that he couldn't do.

My children rang me regularly. They live at the other end of the country so couldn't visit at the best of times, let along during a pandemic. They took it in turns to call me and ensured that I received at least one call a day.

~

Then there are the dark times. These can appear at any time, good or bad. When my children call me, I feel guilty for not being closer to them. If only I was more mobile, I could be a better mother. They say that they are fine, that they don't need me, so maybe they don't. Maybe they would be better off without me; something less for them to worry about. They have their own lives, they are happy and contented, so they don't need me. When they were younger, I did my best for them, but I doubt they had an ideal childhood.

They don't visit us. Their dad is never home and I am here all the time, but I fail to get the house to a decent enough standard for visitors, for anyone really. I can see the look in Tom's eyes when he comes home. He's disgusted by the state of our home. I can almost read his mind. 'There she is, slumped on the sofa as per usual. Lazy cow never does anything. Maybe if Rachael wasn't so fat, she could move around more. Maybe if she cleaned up, that itself would help her lose some weight'. I don't blame him really. There isn't much of a marriage going on here anymore. For years we didn't even see each other because of my inability to stay awake. All I needed to do was get up a bit earlier, but I'm just too lazy. He's disgusted with me, I'm not the woman he married 33 years ago. Back then I was young and spritely. Now I'm fat and useless.

We don't have friends, because of the same reasons. Our house is a mess, and he's never here, but I am here all the time. Tom does occasionally go out to friends' houses during his precious time off. He'd rather visit his friends than spend time with me. I don't blame him really.

Secretly I think he may have another woman, a lover. Sometimes I get angry and accuse him, sometimes I know that he deserves someone better.

I don't think he wears a mask when he visits his 'friends'. He won't catch COVID off me, as I never go out. The carer wears a mask when she comes round, and I have to wear one of those blue disposable ones that she brings for me. But he could catch COVID off one of his friends, if they don't wear masks. And that's how these things start; one person not wearing a mask, then they get too close to someone else who doesn't wear a mask, then they catch the virus. Then he could come home and give it to me. Then anyone who visits me could catch it. Then they could die; we could all die.

When I first heard about COVID I had a panic attack. I think I've watched too many horror films, because I actually thought that loads of people were going to die and then come back as zombies and kill the rest of us.

W hen the depression lifts and I can think clearly, I know that this is all just silly. I know that my husband and children love me, and that they have my best interests at heart. Its just a silly condition that I have that sends the wrong signals to my brain.

Dogmatics

The teenagers had been instructed to form an orderly queue at Miss Jones' desk, once they had completed their task of a story based on just a picture given to each class member at the beginning of term. Isla's picture was of a guillotine with a crowd of people.

There was nothing wrong with a bit of gore, kids these days loved it. Except Isla didn't love it. She had been known to pass out in biology class. Her parents had even complained about a gory horror '15 rated' film that the children had watched in class around Christmas, when even the eldest children were only 14, because a very pale Isla had been sent home from college with a disposable sick bowl.

The complaint was only a small reason for the class to dislike Isla. She had been disliked since she was nine but had no idea why. An only child, there was no-one she could talk to about this. Until recently, she had been able to confide in her best friend, Brooke, but since this academic year began, she had decided to turn against her too. It was then that Isla decided that she would never trust anyone again.

The bullying had started when her family moved to a new city. The first incident was during a lunchbreak in the playground when a girl, Brittany, had decided to pin her up against the railings for the whole hour after they had eaten. They were forced to shake hands and apologise in front of the whole class by their teacher.

From then on, name calling was a daily occurrence; 'dumpling', despite having a very small frame and 'dogmatics' "because you have a face like a dog", were the two main ones that had stuck around for the last five years.

The saddest thing was that Isla had always loved school up until then. She still loved learning, just not the education establishment. Knowing that on a good day she would 'only' have verbal abuse helped her through, as she never knew when or why the physical beating would start.

As all of the children slowly started lining up at the desk, Isla hung back a little. She had assumed that the others didn't like her because she was too keen, so she 'dumbed it down' as much as possible, and as a result her grades went down. The 'Grade A' student was now an 'Average Jo'. That was only one of the many reasons why she waited until a few other of her peers had taken their turn. Another reason was Danyl.

About the same time as the bullying had started, she had discovered him. He picked her up off the floor after a light beating, and she fell in love instantly. Unfortunately, the feeling wasn't mutual.

After about a year, she and her friend, Courtney, discovered that they both loved him, and Courtney insisted that they both go and pay him a visit and ask him if he wanted to 'go out with' either of them. Courtney, tall and beautiful with stunning long blonde hair, knew where he lived, and it wasn't far away. Surprisingly, he turned down both offers, and the girls solemnly walked back home. Courtney shrugged it off in no time, but Isla, who was short, thin with dark pixie-style hair, the total opposite to her only friend, took it to heart.

English was the only lesson that Isla and Dan shared, and

the young girl was too scared to even look at him. She did sneak a quick glance or two when she could, but knew he'd never be interested in her.

Dan was currently second in line to hand in his story about an alien invasion in London, so she decided that she could slip into line while his attention was elsewhere. Brooke was directly before him, and as Isla proceeded to the desk, she was shoulder-shoved, given a dirty look and been told she was a bitch by her former friend. Isla knew to just ignore her, and continued to line up and wait for the teacher. Her head was fuzzy from the incident but she succeeded to hold back her tears. She knew not to provoke Brooke any further, mainly because she knew how violent she could be with people she didn't like, but also because she was now the only person in the whole college who knew about her feelings for Dan.

A few other teens joined the queue after Isla, the one directly behind being Ricky, the only boy who was ever violent to her. This may sound like a relief, but girls fighting with other girls can be very vicious. For the rest of the 10 minutes' wait to see Miss Jones, Ricky kicked Isla's ankles. Constantly.

By the time it was her turn to hand over her story, she had no words, just a sadness in her eyes. She returned to her seat once dismissed and just sat quietly until the end of the lesson. With their teacher's attention diverted, the other pupils had an opportunity to throw scrunched up pieces of paper, pens and even gum as Isla. This was one of the reasons why she had a very short pixie haircut, after someone threw gum at her and it had landed in her hair; as well as nits, of course. As Ricky finished his consultation, he walked back to his desk via Isla's, pushing the furniture into her while doing so.

Soon it was home time, but this wasn't exactly a welcoming treat for Isla, she had to endure the journey first. She lived about half an hour's walk away, and for the first part her route was the same as the majority of the other students.

She automatically walked to and from college with her head down, focusing more on her feet than those in front of her. Her attackers usually combatted her from the rear. When her hair had been longer, it was generally pulled by several girls; that was another reason for the haircut. Name calling was standard; that was the first indication that they were behind her. It was nearly always a 'they', as they walked home in groups.

"Oi, nit head", was a common one. She'd been off college for a few days then suddenly returned with a lot less hair.

"Sket."

"Whore."

"Bitch."

Barking noises, the occasional howl.

Pushing her lightly to keep her on her feet; pushing her so hard so that she'd fall; pushing her into a fence, a garden, a hedge.

Pulling her bag and throwing it on the floor; pulling her bag and emptying everything onto the pavement; pulling her back and throwing it into the road; pulling her bag and throwing it into someone's garden.

Kicking the back of her legs so that she'd stagger; kicking the back of her legs so that she'd fall; kicking the back of her legs so much that she'd need painkillers to sleep and have bruises for weeks.

Throwing things at her. Pens again, maybe pebbles.

Spitting at her.

Wiping their hands in all kinds of unsavoury substances and then smearing it across her face; in her hair; on her clothes.

Some days they 'levelled up', and would pin her against a wall, or hedge, or gate, and hit her. Today was one of those days. Brooke was now part of this small gang of pent up hormones. Brooke's frame was larger than Isla's, but then again, Isla was tiny, in so many ways. She pushed up against Isla, pinning her to the wall of a nearby house. Brooke grew her nails long. This was perfect for scratching Isla's face, neck, chest, back, and this was indeed her contribution to the gang.

"Give me dirty looks, would ya?" the assailant yelled as she punched Isla in the stomach.

Isla fell to the floor.

"Don't get too close to her, B. You don't wanna get nits!" one of the gang members advised the new recruit.

The all-girl gang laughed and walked off, each calling her another name and giving her a swift kick as they passed her. She sat and sobbed as her legs bled from grazes where she had been shoved against the wall; her face and neck wounds stinging from Brooke's fingernails. Her hands were scuffed from where she had stumbled roughly, and small bits of grit were embedded into the skin on the palms.

Isla was an avid reader, but even she knew that no knight in shining armour was going to rescue her, so she dried her eyes and pulled herself back up, retrieving her bag from the homeowner's garden and limping the rest of the way home.

"You should just tell them 'sticks and stones may break my bones, but names will never hurt me,' her mum had advised one afternoon.

She had tried that, and the bullies had rallied round and found twigs and pebbles to do just that.

"Throw your shoe at them," was another piece of golden advice, which Isla had tried after Ricky had finished swinging her around by her hair in front of the lollipop lady, who just stood by and watched, but he had just ran off with it, leaving her to walk home with only one shoe.

Her parents had offered to speak to the head of the college, but experience had taught her that such an act wouldn't end well. She simply kept it all inside, wished she could just die.

Today was no different. As soon as she arrived at home, she dashed upstairs and lay on her bed crying silently. There was a little tap at the door. Isla desperately tried to dry her eyes as her mum entered.

"Hello, Isla," she spoke. "School not good today?"

Isla looked at her mother blankly. Was her face not an

indication?

"Well, it looks like it might get better for you. All schools are closing because of this Corona thing."

Isla sat up at this announcement.

March 30th 2020 became the best day of Isla's life, well, since she was nine, anyway.

Foreshadowing would have told her that she would never fully recover from this life experience. She would probably go through life not trusting people completely and have a lifetime of mental health problems. But for now, life was definitely looking up for her.

Three's Company

"Can we have a sleepover at the weekend, Mummy?" Daisy asked her mum as they walked home from school.

"Only if you promise not to ask in that voice for the rest of the week," her mum, Kelsey laughed.

Daisy beamed at her.

"So does that mean I can too?" Poppy smiled sweetly, ensuring she DIDN'T have a whine in her voice.

'May as well get it over with in one go', Kelsey thought to herself, as she pulled her coat tightly around her neck. She nodded and the girls cried 'yay!'.

They both chattered excitedly all the way home. Once inside, Kelsey made them all hot chocolates and all three sat in front of the TV to watch a film. She knew her girls were spoilt, but she'd rather spoil them any day of the week than risk losing one of them. It had been a close call with Poppy late last year when she had a very bad asthma attack at school and was rushed to hospital. With no father to lean on, she faced the fear that she could lose her eldest daughter alone.

Kelsey had a boyfriend now, and he was so much better than his predecessor, but he worked long hours and was only at home when the girls were at school. This worked fine for her, the kids didn't need a hands-on dad, they'd proved that for most of their lives. She'd always thought she was the clingy kind who would want a full-time boyfriend, but this way she could raise her daughters how she liked without having to answer to anyone else; take someone else's thoughts into consideration. If she wanted to treat her girls to hot chocolate every evening after school in winter, then she could. If she wanted to buy them ice cream after school in summer, the same applied.

Dinner was fishfingers and chips tonight, followed by sticky toffee pudding and custard. Then it would be bath and bed.

Once the girls were all settled in bed, it was adult time. Kelsey poured herself a glass of wine and curled up on the sofa. Tom, her boyfriend was a consultant at the hospital and worked long hours. He didn't like to disturb the young family, so usually slept in the on-call room when not working. He usually tried to call her around 11 p.m., when he had his break, so there was time to watch a film before then. Although she didn't want to revolve her life around a man, she still aimed to stay up until just after his break time, just in case. Sometimes she'd take the phone to bed with her if she was tired.

Tonight's movie was Top Gun. This Tom was much sexier than her's, but beggars can't be choosers. She giggled to herself as she slipped the DVD into the smart TV and poured herself another wine.

***

The week seemed to drag, with Daisy reminding her regularly about the sleepover, even writing a list of food items that they'd eat, although Kelsey was sure she didn't need 3 different types of chocolate each.

As she was usually preoccupied during school hours, she arranged for her mum to pick up the girls after school and spend a little time there while she popped into town to get the treats.

It was a struggle to get out of bed, as Tom was great company, and it would have been OK to take the girls into town the next day to buy the treats, but she was determined to get them herself as the children could be a bit difficult to drag around town, especially on a Saturday, so she kissed her boyfriend goodbye and slipped her clothes back on. Tom's work was in the other direction so he couldn't give her a lift, but she was happy enough to catch a bus.

Generally she didn't like public transport, there were too many virus-ridden passengers in close proximity, but it was too cold and far to walk. The shops weren't too busy, and she managed to pick up snacks and a new DVD in no time. She was just walking to the bus stop so that she could get to her mum's house, when she saw Tom entering a pub on the corner opposite the bus station.

"What is he doing in town?" she muttered to herself.

He stood at the door, holding the door open for a couple of people, and then Kelsey saw a woman kiss him, on the lips! He had no family, from what he had told her, so there would be no-one but her to kiss.

"Are you getting on or what, love?" the driver asked.

She nodded and handed him the money for the ticket, sitting down in a seat where she could see the pub. She could see him sitting down at a table near the window with the people he had just walked in with.

She was so upset that she nearly missed the stop to her mum's house, the bus almost flinging her along the aisle as she stood up and rang the bell. She apologised to the driver, who muttered to himself as he closed the door behind her.

She was close to tears as she reached her mum's house, but held it back once inside, not wanting to worry her family. She chose to not stay for a drink but promised to pop round again next week to catch up. It was dark, so she hurried her daughters home. Mum had fed them, so she sent them straight up to bed. They whined, as they were missing out on their usual hot chocolate and film, but she pointed out that they'd been treated at their gran's and would get more treats with the sleepover.

The following night was trying, as all sleepovers were. Four girls demanding attention and having to compromise rather than getting their own way. Kelsey was already in a bad mood, as not only had Tom been at the pub when he should have been at work, but he hadn't phoned her either. All sorts of thoughts had run through her head, reasons why he hadn't called. He had left on good terms that afternoon, so had no reason to avoid her. He clearly wasn't too busy at work, seeing as he was in a pub.

Her mind had reeled most of the night before, and now she was crabby from being tired as well as Tom's antics. The children were loud and barely slept.

When morning arrived, Kelsey was grateful that the visitors were collected early. Her own two were grumpy and over-tired, so she pushed through the day as best she could, allowing them to re-watch whatever films they wanted but ensuring the stay awake so that they'd sleep later. She fed and bathed them early and sent them to bed.

A whole bottle of wine was consumed that night, as she stared at her phone waiting for it to ring. Midnight came and went and she had broken her own golden rule about staying up for his call. She was angry with herself when she eventually retired to bed, but luckily the wine helped her to drift off and stay asleep.

***

Everything seemed a bit of a daze the following week. She still hadn't heard from Tom on Monday; if she hadn't seen him on Friday then she would have been worried sick about him.

There was general unrest at school as it was announced that schools were closing due to a virus outbreak. Secretly Kelsey hoped for them to close, as she missed them terribly when they were at school. She had always wanted to home school her children, as her school life a been awful. By the time the closure was official she had already started lesson planning.

The next few weeks were a joy for them all. The children kept Kelsey busy, too busy to even think about Tom for the most part. He had called a handful of times, she had ignored each one. Poppy and Daisy flourished at home. They followed the curriculum, which wasn't difficult for key stage one students, most of the time, and as the weather improved they could play out in the garden, study minibeasts, have treasure hunts and even grow vegetables. Ice cream replaced hot chocolate, and they made their own as often as possible.

As the temperatures rose, all three developed colds. As

soon as Kelsey realised that they had some symptoms of the virus she rushed them all into a&e.

"You know that we can't just take everyone in, just because they have the common cold?" the snooty receptionist scolded her from behind her glass screen.

"Poppy has asthma," Kelsey explained.

"That doesn't mean it's COVID, dearie."

"She was in here a few months ago with an asthma attack," Kelsey persisted.

The receptionist tapped on her keyboard. "She was given an inhaler?" she raised her eyes up from the screen.

Kelsey rummaged through her bag. "Yes, yes, I have it here." She held it up to show her.

"So give to her as advised."

"But we all have temperatures," the young mum continued.

"Then take paracetamol then," she sighed.

"I don't have any. Can't a doctor give me a prescription?"

"You want a doctor, who's rushed off their feet with too many patients, most of whom are dying, to write you a prescription for a medicine, which costs the NHS over a hundred pounds, that you can buy for less than a pound?"

Despite this being rhetorical, Kelsey agreed that they deserved this. The receptionist wasn't budging, and the queue was growing behind them.

"Well, can you call their dad please? He's a consultant here, he'll get us seen to."

She gave the receptionist Tom's name and there was a call for him over the intercom. Sure, it was a white lie, and they hadn't spoken for months, but he would help them. They sat in the waiting room, coughing and sneezing, and whining regularly.

"Mum, can we just go home, I don't feel well," Daisy moaned.

"That's why we're here!" Kelsey snapped.

Daisy cried, and her mum comforted her, apologising.

When the queue died down a bit, she stormed over to the receptionist. "Can you call him again please?"

She sighed again and rolled her eyes. "What's his name?"

"Tom Phoenix," Kelsey replied.

The receptionist was back at her computer.

"You could try Thomas, if Tom doesn't work," Kelsey suggested, trying to be helpful.

"I know what Tom is short for," she muttered under her breath. "No, he's not an employee at this hospital." She tapped a bit more, "he's not showing as being an NHS employee at all," she concluded, indicating for her to move out of the way to allow the next patient to get seen to.

Kelsey angrily grabbed her phone from out of her bag and rang Tom. There was no answer. She sat down with the girls and called a taxi to get home, then tried Tom again.

"Hello," he answered.

"Where are you?" she screeched down the phone line.

"I'm at work," he replied quietly.

"Well I'M AT YOUR WORK, AND YOU'RE NOT!!" she replied.

"Did I not tell you that I've been transferred to Coventry? There was an emerg…."

"CUT THE CRAP, TOM. I'VE BEEN DOING A LITTLE INVESTIGATING."

"Can you keep your voice down please. I have very sick patients here!"

"Well, *Mister* Phoenix, you don't exist at this hospital, they have checked their records."

"What is this, Kelsey? I wasn't at the infirmary initially, I was with a private health company. They called upon me to assist. I'm sure if you were to call the Coventry Infirmary…"

"You just talk bullshit, it's all a pack of lies!"

"Look," he spoke through gritted teeth, "I can be with you in about an hour, back at home. Let's talk this over."

"No, don't bother! I got them to check all of the NHS

databases. You don't exist to them!"

"Kels…"

"Your stuff will be in the garage. You can come round to collect it from tomorrow, but don't bother coming in."

"It's my house, you can't st…"

"No, it WAS your home, but it's my name on the tenancy. Since you have found somewhere to sleep for the last few months, I'm sure you will have no trouble."

"I have obviously been sleeping in the on-call rooms betw…."

"Don't wanna hear it!" Kelsey threw the phone across the waiting room. Daisy ran to fetch it, as a security guard escorted them out of the building.

"There are sick, contagious people here," he reprimanded her. "You are risking lives here, whether you have COVID or not. Wait outside for your taxi."

The taxi driver refused to take the family home, as they were displaying too many symptoms, ironically. She rang for another and explained to the taxi controller that they had been checked out by the hospital and had the all-clear. This driver arrived fairly quickly and they were soon home.

Kelsey's anger had dissipated a little by the time they reached home. She took her daughters' temperatures and found that it was within the healthy scale for both of them. She gave them an ice cream each and left them watching TV. She nipped upstairs to her room to calm down.

She decided it was time to take matters into her own hands. Despite his lack of contact over the last few months, her *ex*-boyfriend had still been paying all of her bills and rent, she assumed. It was his bank account, sure, but she hadn't had any unpaid bills arrive, either in her name or his. Nevertheless, she decided to contact various benefit agencies to free her from his control. She had lived with Tom for 4 years and it had been unnecessary for her to get a job. Now she couldn't, due to the pandemic.

The evaluators were very understanding, but told her that they would have to cancel her partner's claim before starting a new one.

"But he's a consultant at a hospital," she explained. "Wouldn't he be earning too much to get anything?"

"I would have thought so, yes," the telephonist agreed, "but it says here that he's your carer. You currently have disability benefits due to your... M.S., it says here on my screen," he continued, tapping away. "I can get the payments for that transferred to your bank account if you have your details handy. If he is no longer your carer, we can cancel that payment and you can advise us of a new carer once you have arranged it. This payment will be backdated to today's date, as long as it's within the next 3 months. There are also tax credits in both your names and your two children, Poppy Jay and Daisy Jay? This will need to be cancelled now that he has moved out, but can be reapplied for. I shall give you the website to do this online, along with your housing benefit claim too, so that you can complete this. The new claim will be fast-tracked, as we are aware that things are difficult for new claimants right now. When did your partner move out?"

Kelsey thought about this for a moment. "I haven't seen him since the weekend before lockdown."

***

Later, finances sorted and all unwanted belongings packed and stored in the garage, Kelsey sat down with her girls and finally relaxed. Life was going to go in a new direction now.

Chain Reaction

Yvette really admired her bosses.

Louanne Marshall had started her business from scratch, by first offering to answer telephone calls for her friend, Sian Murphy, who found work too busy to answer the calls herself. Sian was a very admirable businesswoman herself. Copy typing for other busy businesspeople, she didn't want to be disturbed by phone calls, as her clients paid her by the hour, and efficiency was essential.

Their company, 'MM', which represented their surname initials plus the year they merged their businesses, 2000, had thrived and expanded over the last 20 years. They now had a staff of 10 telephonists, audio typists and a marketing assistant.

Yvette had also been there from the beginning too, hired to clean their offices. It was just a 'little job', a couple of hours a night.

Dean, her husband was the assistant manager at a local fast-food restaurant in town. His hours varied from week to week, as the eatery was open long hours. He started working there when he was 16.

He'd been more than happy to leave work at 16, as most of his friends did too, except they all found jobs they were happy with. Dean, however, just saw a sign for vacancies when he was passing by one day, and popped in on the off-chance and was hired straight away.

It wasn't one of the famous fast-food restaurants that were popping up everywhere. Wages were low, started at £30 a week as a part-time lunch-time server, but had worked his way up to the current role, although it had taken 20 years! It wasn't that he wasn't capable, but there were just no opportunities to be promoted when there were only 4 staff there! It was enough for him as a teenager, he managed to afford to pay board and have a pint or two with the lads at the weekend.

Then one day he met Yvette. The attraction was instant. She walked into the restaurant during the busiest time of day, on the busiest day of the week – Saturday! The queue from the football fans who wanted chips for the walk to the stadium was taking its toll on Dean, the only one working there. Yvette, bold as brass, pushed through the crowds of rowdy men and walked behind the counter, ready to serve. Two hours of non-stop counter service and the waiting line finally dissipated.

From that moment on, they were attached at this hip. They moved as one, both at work, where Yvette had been hired immediately, and at home. They had moved in together within a few short weeks. Money was tight, but they were used to that. Their parents had lived on the breadline, as had their parents, and their parents, and so on. However, they weren't expecting to hear the pitter patter of tiny feet within a year, reducing their wages by half again.

Eventually, Dean managed to secure more hours at work, but money was still tight. Having children turned out to a blessing in more than one way. Any money Dean was unable to earn, was partly topped up by the government.

Dean was the main wage earner of the family, as Yvette focussed on nurturing their children. They learned to survive on the small income they received, which meant they needed to cut out some luxuries, such as the weekly boys' night out. But they were happy. Yvette had attempted to work when the children were younger but found herself unreliable whenever illness struck the household. She became an expert at bookkeeping, for the family's finances at least.

As the children grew up, Yvette was able to leave the younger children with her eldest son, Aaron, who appreciated the 'little job' he now had, and the little extra cash he received. He had 'acquired' a girlfriend recently, and he could now afford to treat her to little things.

Yvette hoped that one day she could be as successful as Sian and Louanne. Her plan was to take on more clients who needed their offices or houses cleaned, until she was working as many hours as she wanted to; earning what she wanted. In the interim, MM was the perfect place to work.

Then the lockdown hit!

"The government says we have to all work from home," Louanne started, as she faced a sea of uncertain faces. "But don't fret, we are going to ensure that each of you receives all the equipment that you need to continue to work for us. Those of you who work the phones, you will get a VOIP phone. These phones will all be enabled to run off your existing broadband services. Once government funding is confirmed, we will give you each a small additional allowance to cover the utilities that will increase as a result.

"If any of you are likely to struggle by working from home, please come and see me after this meeting, whether it is finding a quiet space, affording the utility bills before we get the funding, or anything else that may cause an issue. We don't expect any reduction in our clients' services, they will still need people answering their phone calls.

"If you could all now go and pack, then meet me back in my office, please."

Sian smiled nervously, waiting for them to leave. "This just leaves the copy typists. The same rules apply. We will distribute a laptop to each of you who are still able to work. At present, we are not sure how this lockdown will affect our side of the business. We will need to speak to each of our clients, to see how this affects them and their workload.

"Like with Louanne, please let me know if working from home is likely to be an issue. The government is talking about possibly subsidising those who cannot work from home, but it will only cover a percentage of wages. I'm not sure what that is or when it will be. BUT I must have complete honesty from you; if you can still work, please do so professionally. Don't say that you can't, as it could have a diverse affect on our lives. This is serious shit, pardon my French!

"If you think that you can't work from home, for the same reasons that Louanne mentioned, please don't say that you can, as that will have a negative affect too. I am here for you all. If any of you need any advice or support, I will do my **utmost** to find a solution.

"Now off you all go, pack up your stuff and then meet me back here, please."

Everybody left.

Everybody except for Yvette.

She shifted uncomfortably as Sian started clearing away the dirty mugs and leftover breakfast pastries that they had provided for the staff meeting.

"I can do that for you, Sian," Yvette broke the silence.

Sian gasped; she hadn't realised that anyone was still there. Yvette walked up to her and took the dirty pots from her hands.

"What about me?" Yvette probed. "If everyone is at home, there'll be no offices to clean."

"Ummm...." Sian replied, "just stay here for now, and once everyone else has gone we can have a chat with Louanne."

"Sure, I'll wash these pots up then," Yvette smiled.

The washing up took a lot less time up than 10 employees packing up their belongings, collecting equipment, signing release forms for the equipment and general queries, so Yvette sat patiently in the kitchen, nibbling on leftover pastries.

Once the last of the staff had left, she wandered back into Sian's office. The two entrepreneurs were still discussing the events of the day.

"Hi," she spoke quietly, worried that she was interrupting.

"Oh hi, Yvette," Louanne greeted her. "We hadn't

forgotten you," she lied.

"The situation is just a bit different for you, Yvette," Sian continued. "You are cash in hand, so the government don't even know that you work here. Remember when you first started and you said that it wasn't worth it financially if it was 'on the books' as anything you earned would be taken off you in benefits?"

The was a long pause.

"Once we know the funding we get from the government, we will know more and be able to update you."

They all left the office and went in their different directions.

Back at home, Yvette was ready to cry as she unlocked the front door to her home, but was startled by a hive of activity. Dean and the children were all their waiting for her.

Jadie ran to her mum excitedly, "School's closed," she squealed with delight.

"Oh!" was all that Yvette could muster.

It was a light at the end of a tunnel in a way. She loved to be with her children, and was one of those mothers who cried on their first day at school and at the end of the school holidays.

"Lauren is already in her room," Dean announced. "She was so excited that she just ran straight up there and was on her games console in a matter of moments."

Yvette walked up to her partner and kissed him on the cheek. "I'm so sorry you had to pick them up from school, I had to go in for a meeting."

"I've been sacked," he whispered into her ear before she pulled away.

Her face dropped. "I don't understand?"

"They said they were just going to close down, as they couldn't afford to survive the lockdown," he explained.

"Sian and Louanne said that they should be getting some funding from the government to cover wages," Yvette replied, "so shouldn't you?"

Dean shrugged. "I just don't know. That's good that they will still be able to pay you some, though."

Yvette shook her head and looked down at her worn-down trainers. "It doesn't include me, as I was just cash in hand."

"I'm never going to see Jana again," Aaron blurted out, emerging from the kitchen.

"It won't last forever, Aaron," Yvette comforted, not fully knowing what would happen. "You can still text her and message her on the internet, can't you?"

"Ain't got credit to text her," he replied.

"Well then, just message her."

Once her son had left the room, dragging his schoolbag upstairs, she turned back to Dean. "I'm sure we will be ok. Once I've had a coffee, I shall take a look on the computer and see what financial help we can get."

She sat at the dining table with her coffee and an opened envelope and started to do her usual household calculations. 'Benefits calculator' she typed into the bar at the top of the web browser. Tapping in their income, which would now be zero, she discovered that they were already in receipt of the maximum amount of Universal Credit. She already knew that her wages would just be lost, that was a given, but as Dean had been fired, rather than whatever the government was going to call the situation of thousands of people, it appeared he wasn't entitled to anything to replace his loss of earnings.

She tapped the pen onto the scrap paper she was doodling on. She needed to calculate how they could afford to live with the funds that they had remaining. She had already tightened their budget a few times in their 16 years together, like when they first lived together, when Yvette couldn't work due to morning sickness, when they had to move to a bigger home for their expanding family.

She had already cut down on the heating by only switching it on just before everyone woke up, until they left for work or school, then switching it on for just a few hours in the evening. It was currently the end of March, and everyone would be at home. Thank goodness they had jumpers and thick socks, as that would now be a necessity; she wasn't sure if she could still afford to have the heating on at all, despite it still being a very chilly March.

Electricity wasn't cheap. She could cut costs by handwashing clothes and sweeping instead of hoovering.

Food. For years she had resorted to off cuts of meat, the fatty stuff as it was cheaper. Potatoes were always a cheap option, as was pasta. She would just have to make these foods stretch further. They'd need to have non-branded products like fishfingers with unknown fish in; burgers, with unknown cuts of meat, if there's any meat in them at all.

'How am I going to shop for food if everywhere is closed?' she thought.

Even if shops were open, public transport would be cancelled, the internet was telling her. Maybe online shopping would be ok. She tried supermarkets' websites, starting with the cheapest. 'NO SLOTS AVAILABLE'. 'ONLY AVAILABLE FOR VULNERABLE HOUSEHOLDS, LIKE THE DISABLED OR ELDERLY'.

Ok, so she'd have to walk when the time came. 'It would be ok', she assured herself, knowing that it probably wouldn't.

***

The days went by, and food supplies were diminishing. Shopping was possible, as long as it was only 1 person per household, and they MUST wear a face mask. Where was she supposed to get a mask from? She found an online video showing her how to make one. She felt a bit of a prat walking round with half a bra attached to her face, but needs must and all that.

After queueing for 95 minutes, she eventually managed to get into the nearest supermarket. The hand sanitiser that they provided stung the cuts and dry skin on her hands, caused by all that handwashing she had done recently.

Yvette followed the arrows stuck on the floor obediently. There were signs everywhere, telling their customers to stay at least two metres apart. No Pasta, no pasta sauce, no fishfingers or burgers, no toilet roll. Only the expensive 'organic' milk. No bread. No flour to make her own.

No cheap (or expensive) mince, whether it was beef, pork or turkey. Empty fridges and freezers everywhere, with all products sitting side by side in one appliance; plenty of salmon and beef joints, £15 each, just for the small ones. £35 for a largeish whole salmon! She had managed to make a roast chicken last for 3 days' worth of meals in the past, but there were none of them either, and the beef wouldn't feed her hungry lot for one meal, let alone three.

She stood to one side, allowing others to pass by her where possible and retrieved her purse from her bag. She had £20 in £1 coins, which she had been saving in an old gravy pot in the food cupboard. She didn't know what to do. She couldn't ring Dean for advice, as her credit had expired. She walked around the store again, desperately looking for inspiration. Nothing. She walked home, empty-handed.

Four hungry faces greeted her when she got home.

"Internet's gone, Mum, so I can't contact Jana at all anymore."

"Surely this situation can't go on for much longer?" she muttered to her family. "It's already been a month!"

Once Bitten

"You ruin everything! You could have just said that you didn't want to go to the party, and then I could have gone sooner. But nooooo, you have to wait until the last minute to change your mind! Well, I'm going without you. HAPPY NEW YEAR, NOT!!"

Jessica waited until Shaun had left, slamming the door so hard that the whole flat shook, before she cried her heart out. Her health had taken a dramatic decline this last year. She had collapsed at a meeting a few months ago, and was still undergoing tests to find out what exactly was going on.

She picked at her latest scar on her calf until it bled. Probably wasn't a good idea, as it had already become infected once. The surgeon was sure to give her a telling off for it, but that wasn't for a few weeks yet, so it'd heal with plenty of time – if she left it alone long enough to let it heal!

She turned on the tv, but everything was celebration and fireworks. She did want to go to Shaun's friend's party, but he had gone for a nap that afternoon and overslept. Jess had nodded off on the sofa herself, and only woke up when she heard her husband storming around. Unlike 'normal' people, it took Jess a little longer to wake up after any amount of sleep, so had been groggy for the confrontation. She hadn't even said that she didn't want to go, it was merely the fact that she wasn't as awake as he was, or dressed up yet, plus the fact she hadn't woken him up.

The tv blared to itself as Jessica waded through quite a few tissues with her sobbing, which didn't cease until just before midnight. It hadn't been the first New Year's Eve that she had been alone. Shaun had a habit of causing a scene every year, he didn't understand how much she hated it when it was his favourite time of the year. The fact was that every year something bad happened on that date; her Gran had died a few years back, she had experienced quite a few breakups with exes, who had chosen to take a new woman out instead.

"You can't hold onto that shit forever," she had been told.

Memories are memories as far as Jess was concerned.

***

She awoke the next day to the slamming of the front door. Luckily, Shaun had a hangover, so just went straight upstairs to bed, whereas she had fallen back to sleep on the sofa. 'Roll on Monday', she thought, 'we'll both be back at work then!' She did her best to stay out of the way for the time being, migrating to alternative rooms when Shaun entered them. She knew she couldn't avoid him forever, but this would suffice for now.

Her smartphone became her best friend, as she secretly started to look online for alternative places to live. Even the prices of the smallest flats were beyond her reach though, let alone the hefty deposits and bonds, plus she had no references or guarantors to fall back on. Something would come up, she was sure. She would just have to keep looking.

***

Monday brought the peace of work. She didn't *love* her

job, but it paid the bills and provided a sanctuary away from home. Shaun only worked part-time at a local pizza restaurant in the evenings, as he was studying for his 'A' Levels during the day, so Jess was the main wage earner. She didn't mind, as he had supported her when she couldn't work due to illness the other year. Work was certainly better than staying at home, as Shaun was at home much of the time, his college course only lasting around 12 hours a week. The worst part of work was the journey to and from, as Shaun was the driver of the house. Jess hated his driving, scared her silly with the last-minute brakes and diving into bus lanes to avoid traffic, to ensure that she wasn't late.

Jess knew that she wasn't well liked at work, although she had no idea why. Sure, she hated herself at times, so why shouldn't others, but she didn't know if there was a specific reason. Nevertheless, she wasn't treated badly, they were still civil to her. Just nothing 'clicky'.

She handed in a letter to HR, to show that she had a follow-up appointment with her surgeon in a few weeks and went to make the drinks for her office colleagues. Everyone's drinks requirements were on a board in the kitchen, but Jess knew them off by heart. She put a smile on her face as she walked back to her desk, distributing the drinks on the way.

Work always flew by as it was busy, and again Jess was left waiting for Shaun to pick her up, dreading the journey home. She did her best to stay quiet in the car, it was easier that way. However, with Shaun she couldn't win, no matter what. If she talked, she was snapped at, if she didn't, she was berated for being hostile.

Once at home, she gave the place a quick clean and prepared dinner. They ate in silence, and Jess was grateful when Shaun left for work shortly after. Once he had left, she trawled through the internet for flats, even flat shares would be better than living here.

***

Their wedding anniversary was in February. Yes, they were one of the stupid ones who chose Valentine's Day for their wedding. 'What a joke!' Jess thought, but was grateful that Shaun had work that day. His employers had been messing round with his wages for a few months now, it seemed that no matter how many hours he worked, he still only earned the equivalent of one evening shift, so it was a welcome relief when he decided to work on that day, rather than request the day off like he usually did.

"I'm sure you understand," he had said.

Oh boy, did she! Jess usually went round to visit her friend, Jane, who was at home alone too. Well, not quite alone, as Jane had a toddler at home.

Jess longed for a child of her own, but Shaun had told her to wait until he had finished his studies and had a decent job first, so that he was financially able to support the family. This had been all that had kept her hanging onto Shaun's arm, hope. Jane's daughter, Molly, was a delight, and the love that Jess couldn't give to her own child she gave to her instead.

Jane was virtually the only friend that Jess had. They enjoyed a giggle and a day of eating whatever they wanted, without Shaun breathing down her neck counting calories. Jess had struggled with her weight for many years, possibly due to comfort eating when things were bad at home. Chinese food was their chosen takeaway most weeks, along with a couple of bottles of wine. Jess usually slept over at Jane's house too, so Shaun didn't have to worry about picking her up.

"I'm leaving him, Jane," Jess blurted out, over a chicken ball and glass of wine.

Jane stared at her blankly, before smiling broadly. "About time too!" she exclaimed.

"I'm looking for places to live right now, but obviously it's not going to be a quick process due to finances and lack of references."

Jane was quiet for a few minutes. "I think I may have a plan for you. Leave it with me!"

Jess was intrigued, but knew that further probing wouldn't help; Jane wasn't good under pressure of any kind.

***

A few days later, at work, Jess received a text message from Jane.

'I'm movin house after my hol nxt mnth, n the landlord said u can hve my place if u like?'.

'OMG', Jess replied. 'U dint tell us u were movin? Where u goin?'.

'Voldemort' she replied.

'Voldemort' was the nickname that they had for Jane's boyfriend. She didn't really discuss it with Jess much, so they named him after 'he who shall not be named' (Harry Potter).

'WOW! Hes fnly commitin??'.

'Yh lol'.

Jane had a lovely little 2 bedroomed house, not an unreasonable price, a perfect fresh start for Jess.

***

Life continued as normal, except Jess attempted to sort out her belongings and pack discreetly. There was nowhere to store it until Jane moved out, but her landlord had confirmed the go-ahead as of 3rd April, a couple of days before Jane was to move in with her boyfriend.

The weeks dragged by, as Jess attempted to keep this massive secret from her husband. She didn't trust anyone at work enough to share the news, so it was all stored in her head. Working out costs, when to pack, what to pack; such excitement but also nerve-racking. All the packing would be done during the last week, while Shaun was away on his annual ski trip with his 'muckers', as Jess called them. For the last few years he had brought her a gift home that had clearly been bought from the airport, but this year she didn't even think he'd bother with that.

She had bought some flat-packed cardboard boxes and hidden them behind the wardrobe. The new house already had basic kitchen appliances, and she would just sit on a deck chair and sleep on a mattress on the floor until she could afford more furniture. She didn't care, as long as she could move!

Five days before the move was a monumental occasion; if Jess had friends, she'd have had a party! Instead, she just sat patiently and waited for Shaun to pack all of his skiing clothes and get the hell out of her way.

She waited. And waited. And waited.

He sat watching tv in the living room, quite chilled out enjoying his favourite sitcom. Jess looked at the calendar on her phone; yes definitely the right day according to her notes. She stood up and went into the kitchen to check the calendar hanging on the wall next to the fridge. Yes, definitely the right day. Maybe it was a late flight.

The clock ticked slower and slower.

Jess woke early the next morning on the sofa; she must have fallen asleep. She made herself a cup of tea and then planned what she would pack and when. The van was booked for 3rd April, moving day, and Shaun was due back on the 5th. Perfect!

"Not working today?" Shaun entered the room.

Jess was taken aback. "I thought you were going skiing," she blurted.

"Cancelled," he replied, pushing past her to get to the kettle.

'Shit!' she thought. 'Time to reassess'.

Jess consulted the calendar again, focussing on previous

weeks. Shaun's college was on Wednesdays and Fridays. His work was on Fridays, Saturdays and Sundays. The van was booked for this Friday, and she knew that he would be out all day, as he went straight from college to work. She just needed time to pack and somewhere to store her belongings in the interim. She called the landlord of Jane's house, but he told her that there was no leeway as he had arranged for his 'maintenance people' to go in and give the place a fresh lick of paint and a routine clean.

Ok, so she knew she could pack her stuff on Wednesday while Shaun was at college; she decided that she would have to just bite the bullet and tell her husband that she was leaving. It would be two days of hell, but in the long run it would be worth it.

***

Then the lockdown hit!

The first Jess knew of it was a call from the removal team, telling her that they had to cancel her booking as they weren't allowed to work.

Suddenly, everyone was either working from home or unemployed, with the exception of a few fast-food places and 'heroes'. Unfortunately, Shaun's work didn't stay open and all of the colleges and schools shut, so this resulted in both him and Jess at home.

Jess's employers were unable to offer work to their employees, so they were all just sent home 'on leave' until further notice.

On what would have been moving day, they received a

call from Jane on the landline. She was left stranded on holiday, unable to get a flight home. As idyllic as this sounded, the tour company was unhelpful and the accommodation situation out there was unsure.

"Just calm down, Jane," she could hear Shaun reassuring her. "We will get this sorted."

Jess hovered around, waiting to speak to her on the phone. Shaun waved her away. He took some details for her and said he would 'make a few calls'. He hung up before giving Jess time to talk to her. This was typical of Shaun, an element of needing control of what she could and couldn't have.

He grabbed his laptop and settled down on the sofa, flicking through different websites including the travel agency that Jane arranged her holiday with. The more places he contacted, the more annoyed he became.

The landline rang again. Shaun was up from his seat before it had registered with Jess. Normally, with Jess being at work all day, she never noticed that her landline was even still connected. In fact, she didn't know for sure if she had known it was connected before Jane rang.

He reeled off all of the information that he had managed to sort so far. "Yes, you will have to stay there longer, but I can give you money if you need it. No, no there's no flights at all. At least you can do the slopes with a two-metre gap."

'The slopes?' Jess thought. 'She went to Ibiza with her mates, I saw her new bikini that she bought. There's no slopes there, is there?'

She knew that there were countries that you could sunbathe in AND go skiing in too, but was sure Ibiza wasn't one of them.

"Yes, I will make sure Molly is ok. We will get it sorted. Hmmm, yes, you too."

It was then, at that moment, that Jess put the pieces together. Shaun was 'Voldemort!'

***

Over the next few weeks, Jess and Shaun were forced to tolerate each other. Her fury at the affair he'd been having with her best friend never subsided. In fact, it only got worse.

Then, suddenly it disappeared completely.

She didn't want to be with Shaun, and he didn't want to be with her. She no longer slammed doors or made snide comments whenever they were in the same room.

Jane returned from her extended holiday, but Shaun couldn't visit her. Everyone was miserable, but it didn't have to be that way.

As the weather got warmer, the clothes got skimpier. Sunbathing in the garden replaced sitting at a desk in front of a computer for seven and a half hours a day.

Hate turned to tolerance.

Tolerance turned to sociable.

Sociable turned to friendliness.

Friendliness turned into like.

Like blossomed into love.

By the end of June, lockdown was over. Shaun had no interest with Jane anymore.

Jane, unaware of the changes in her lover's and best friend's relationship, assumed that she could soon move in with Shaun. But phone calls and texts were ignored.

One day, Jane appeared on their doorstep, bags packed and a small removal van outside. Shaun and Jess were still in bed when she arrived; Jess answered the door wrapped in just a sheet. The two women looked at each other blankly. Jess invited her adversary in, without saying a word, and returned to her bedroom. The van driver started removing all of Jane's belongings out onto the front of the house. A thud sounded from nearby. It was Jess, now dressed simply in one of the summer dresses that had enticed her husband back into their marital bed, with an extremely large box. Opening the front door, she signalled the van driver just as he was leaving. He carried the box to the van. Jess removed the front door key from her keyring, closed the door and headed to her new home, which had been ready for her for the last 3 months.

Four's a Crowd

The sun streaked through the part-opened curtains and almost blinded me. There was nothing quite like afternoon sex; kid-free, uninterrupted coitus. Kelsey had fallen straight to sleep after, but this would only be a nap, as her children would need collecting from school in around forty minutes. That would be my cue to leave. I've never been able to stand children. Luckily my wife and I's children were fully-grown and had moved out.

Oh, maybe I should clarify. Kelsey isn't my wife, she's my lover; girlfriend; partner. The kids? Oh they were around long before I was. Kelsey and I have been together for four years, the kids are six and eight. Annoying little shits, from all accounts. You only have to look at the crayon on the walls, the toys that stray out of the bedroom onto the landing floor. That pain of treading on a piece of Lego is not overexaggerated, it's up there with when I broke my leg. Well, I haven't broken my leg really, it was an excuse I came up with to avoid the six-week school holiday last summer.

I'd been 'away with business' that summer, 'working' in Scotland when I crashed my car. There was no need for Kelsey to come to see me, besides, it wasn't practical with the children being off school. She sent me a handmade 'get well soon' card that her kids made.

In truth, I'd been with my wife for part of this, and with Sally for another part. Sally also has children, but they are shared between her and her ex. When her ex has them, I go round; when they come home, they usually disappear into their bedrooms; teenagers aren't too bad at times.

As a result, I worked 'shifts', depending on who I visited and when. It can get complicated really quickly. My 'time off' with Kelsey is usually 9.30 a.m. to 2.30 p.m., Monday to Friday. Sometimes her kids stay with their grandparents at the weekend, so my hours can be adjusted to suit. I usually 'pop home' in between shifts at the hospital, as I'm a doctor, you see; well, consultant, to be precise. Very, very important. I'm a specialist in spasticity. That sounds rude, I know, not very p.c., but really it means that I work with people who suffer from muscle weakness.

Kelsey suffers from M.S., apparently. I met her when she was visiting her physiotherapist. She was registered in a different hospital so she couldn't be my patient, unfortunately. I had been visiting the hospital for some training. No, I wasn't being trained, of course, I'm the highest level in my field. I was a guest speaker, and I literally bumped into Kelsey in the corridors. She had the most amazing brown eyes, like puppy dog eyes. At first she kept referring to me as Dr Phoenix. I corrected her at first, more as a joke than anything, to *Mr* Phoenix, as I had attended university for longer than the mere doctors, which is why I was a consultant, a specialist, so I was Mr rather than Dr.

Once Kelsey leaves for the school run, I head back to 'work'. By the time I have travelled from one county to the next, Sally has finished work and has a few hours spare before her kids come home from their dad's house, friends' or afterschool clubs. This had been the arrangement long before I met Sally and I slotted in quite easily. What's even better is that they stay at their dad's for the majority of the weekend too, which works well with my shifts at the airport. Four days on and three days off is the norm as a pilot, so Friday through to Sunday I stay at home, with Sally. She's a carer and has to pop to clients' houses during the weekend, but that's not a problem; you can't be in each other's pockets all the time.

After I leave Sally's on Sunday nights, I head home; as in my home with my wife. Rachael, my wife, suffers from M.E., apparently. She struggles to get up and move around generally. If she could just make the effort, she could improve her health without the need for all the prescription medication she takes. These drugs simply exasperate her 'fatigue'. I'm more inclined to diagnose her as lazy; stuck in a rut.

I often tell her that she just needs to fight through the 'pain' that she says that she has, just a little exercise every day would get her body moving. Sure, it would hurt at first, but the secret is to keep moving with M.E. It's highly overrated in my professional opinion. M.E. was known as 'yuppy flu' back in the 80s and that hits the nail on the head; over-privileged people feeling tired, getting stuck in a rut then finding themselves not being able to break the chain.

I first met Rachael when I was dropping off her prescription. I'm a freelance delivery driver for local pharmacies (and a local pizza restaurant as well now), and she became 'too frail' to collect her prescriptions herself. She looked so vulnerable when she answered the door looking dishevelled with her robe half on and her hair flattened on one side. I was hooked. We moved in together not long after that. I've always been a sucker for a lost soul, a damsel in distress.

Kelsey roused slightly from her siesta, rolled over and smiled at me. Generally I didn't think I had a favourite, but if I had to choose, it would be right here, like this. So peaceful and serene. Kelsey was the most beautiful of them all. If it wasn't for the kids, this would be perfect.

"Mmmmmnn, what time is it? "she enquired.

"Almost 2.30," I replied.

"Shame, wish we had time for seconds, "she smiled lustfully.

"There's always time for seconds," I laughed, rolling her over.

"No, the children…."

"I can drive you to school on my way back to work," I insisted.

Thirty-five minutes later we were in the car outside the school gates.

"They'd love to see you again, Tom," she announced as she unclicked her seatbelt.

I shook my head, tapped my watch, gave her a quick kiss and she exited the car.

I'd met them at Christmas last year, when they had returned early from their gran's house because one of them was ill. There's only one thing worse than kids and that is sick kids. Or kids with really noisy toys. Kelsey had gone overboard last year and bought so many electronic toys for them, plus musical instruments. They are such spoilt little girls.

I had a brainwave and offered to pop out and get more batteries as 'they don't last long enough'. Once I had escaped, I nipped round to Sally's earlier than expected, but late enough to catch just the tail end of her kids as they were packing away their bits ready to visit their absent father.

Absent fathers really weren't that bad – they had their good points!

Once they had left, Sally had a couple of clients to visit and then she was all mine, during which time I had rang Kelsey to let her that there was an emergency at work that I had to attend to. It was here that I was heading to now.

Sally has disabled clients that she visits as their carer, and usually arrives home a little later than me, but that gives me the opportunity to have a shower while she is out. I could smell Kelsey on me still and as much as I like it, I didn't want Sally to be suspicious. I grabbed my little suitcase out of the boot of the car and walked up the path, clicking the lock on my key fob. Once indoors, I popped my clothes into the washer, including those I was wearing and headed straight for the shower, butt naked.

Once successfully de-Kelsey'd, I slipped into a pair of jeans and a t-shirt. I switched the clothes from the washer to the dryer and settled down at the table with a coffee from the machine that Sally had pre-set for me.

Sally was my second favourite. She appreciated how hard I worked to support us and made sure I was well looked after upon my return. I could smell the chilli in the slow cooker simmering away for later. She was usually home by around 6pm, and we would eat fairly soon after.

Depending on the quantity of food and how tired we were, we'd either sit and watch TV for a while or go to bed early.

My next flight is usually scheduled for around midnight, so I pack up my washed clothes into my little flight bag and leave at around 11.00 p.m. Today was no different, and I kissed her goodbye after we had finished watching some random film that I wasn't really paying attention to, and left.

It's a short drive from Sally's to home, with Rachael, and I usually arrive around 11.30 p.m., just as my pizza delivery shift finishes.

Rachael responded to her so-called 'illness' completely different to Kelsey. Kelsey maintains a 'normal' life, fighting through her pain, whereas Rachael doesn't; she generally gets up after I've left for work and is in bed by the time I get home. At least I don't have to deal with her shit all the time. I can usually move freely in the bedroom without her waking as her medication is very strong. I have suggested that it should be reduced to give her a better quality of life, like Kelsey does, but Rachael seems content to let her life just drift on by. I leave again at around 8.30 a.m. for my day job at the control centre that the health centres call to arrange deliveries, or rather to give me time to travel over to Kelsey's, and so the cycle continues.

When lockdown hit, I must admit that I panicked briefly.

As a consultant I was reassigned to help out with all the COVID-19 patients that were admitted. Kelsey totally understood that I couldn't be there as often; I was now on duty 24/7.

As a delivery driver, both employers still needed me as much as before, so I carried on with the same routine with Rachael.

However, the sticky issue was with Sally. Flights had been cancelled so I was at a loose end. This wasn't a problem as I loved staying at our house. It was chilled and relaxed; the teenagers, Corey and Shay were rarely out of their rooms.

Sally generally worked from 10 a.m. to 5 p.m. but we'd eat a lovely breakfast in bed together before she left for the day and the kids would join us at the dining table for dinner in the evenings.

The issue was regarding my schedule with Rachael. I couldn't exactly pop out at night and be back in the morning anymore, as Sally would notice! I mulled this over for a while. I decided that I would check up on her in the daytime when Sally was at work.

This overall plan worked well for several weeks. Spending more time with Rachael wasn't as bad as I expected. I started to realise how vulnerable, how ill she actually was, but together we started to work on getting her to reduce her medication to improve her quality of life. I'd get her to walk around a little to get her muscles stronger, and then we would sit and eat lunch together on her good days.

My reason for being with her at a different time of day was because the hospitals were now sending out emergency drugs to those who were ill at home, rather than them being admitted and overwhelming their resources, and this was a 24/7 role shared between a few of us. She never asked about my pizza job or when I slept, so I just kept the momentum going and hoped that her brain fog would stay the same.

Corey had a games console and I allowed him to connect it up to the TV in the living room. All three of us took turns playing multi-player games while Sally was at work. When we weren't playing games, we would watch horror films, and I found us really bonding. We'd chat about all of the destinations I had visited with work, and I promised them that I would try and arrange more holidays for us all, as a family. It was a choice between Egypt or Florida, apparently; sounded good to me. Sally was happy that I was bonding with her kids more and we were spending more time together as a family.

***

Life was very strange now though. It was the same humdrum life every day. Get up – have breakfast – Sally goes to work – I go home to see Rachael -we both get home – have dinner – go to bed.

Occasionally Kelsey would ring me.

"Surely you should be able to come home for a rest once in a while," she would moan at me.

"Babe, I can't risk coming home in case I bring the virus home with me, or take the virus back to work. There are sick, vulnerable people here."

"But we haven't been out to catch anything, and besides, if they're already sick with COVID, then they can't be more infected. Can they?"

I thought for a few minutes. "We don't yet know if I could

pass it to you guys though. I don't want you all to be ill unnecessarily."

"Life is so slow and boring though. The kids are here ALL the time, I just need a break and to see another adult."

'Exactly!' I thought to myself.

I much prefer Sally's kids to Kelsey's! Sally was starting to become my favourite now, with all this time we were spending together. No complications. No stress. No hassle.

One day we were sitting in the garden eating breakfast when I received a call from Kelsey. I chose to ignore it at first, but it became more persistent. I made my excuses and nipped back into the house.

"Where are you?" she screeched down the phone line.

"I'm at work," I replied as quiet as possible, so as not to be overheard.

"Well I'M AT YOUR WORK, AND YOU'RE NOT!!" she replied.

'Think quickly, Tom'. "Did I not tell you that I've been transferred to Coventry? There was an emerg…."

"CUT THE CRAP, TOM. I'VE BEEN DOING A LITTLE INVESTIGATING."

"Can you keep your voice down please. I have very sick patients here!"

"Well, *Mister* Phoenix, you don't exist at this hospital, they have checked their records."

"What is this, Kelsey?" I replied, struggling to process this. "I wasn't at the infirmary initially, I was with a private company. They called upon me to assist. I'm sure if you were to call the Coventry Infirmary…"

"You just talk bullshit, it's all a pack of lies!"

"Look," I spoke through gritted teeth, "I can be with you in about an hour, back at home. Let's talk this over."

"No, don't bother! I got them to check all of the NHS databases. You don't exist to them!"

"Kels…"

"Your stuff will be in the garage. You can come round to collect it from tomorrow, but don't bother coming in."

"It's my house, you can't st…"

"No, it WAS your home, but it's my name on the tenancy. Since you have found somewhere to sleep for the few months, I'm sure you will have no trouble."

"I have obviously been sleeping in the on-call rooms betw…."

"Don't wanna hear it!"

The phone cut off.

I looked round to see that there was no-one around me and went to the bathroom to pull myself together.

I returned downstairs to find Sally clearing away the breakfast stuff.

"Everything OK?" she smiled at me.

I nodded. "It was work. Apparently they are going to start needing us to come in as we are going to be bringing holidaymakers home from other countries."

"Oh," she replied, "I've kind of got used to having you around all the time now, but it's good that you can get back to work, and good that others will be able to come home."

I nodded again. She started to get ready for work, kissing me on the cheek as she passed me. I sat down at the table to gather my thoughts. I sipped my coffee and rubbed my temples. She came back downstairs, kissed me on the cheek again and left.

The kids appeared not long after and they were soon slumped in front of the big screen, shooting each other with controller guns. My phone rang again. It was an unknown number. I rarely answered the phone as it was, let alone from those numbers that were withheld. I let it go through to my answer machine. No message left, their loss. I sat down with the boys and played with them for a while until Kelsey was out of my mind.

The phone rang again, and this time there was a voicemail. I left the boys to their game and moved to the kitchen to listen to it. As I clicked the button to listen, the phone rang again and I had inadvertently answered it. Shit!

"Hello?"

"Is this Mr Phoenix?"

My heart sank. Only Kelsey used that name.

"Who is this?" I asked.

"This is the department for Work and Pensions. We can't give any further information until we have confirmed a few details with you."

My mind racing, I answered the questions swiftly.

"Thank you, Mr Phoenix. We have been contacted by your girlfriend, Miss Jay. She has just been in contact with us to make a claim for benefits, now that you have moved out. However, we have found a claim already active at that address in your name. She was rather alarmed to discover that there was claim for Working and Child Tax Credits, Personal Independent Payments, Housing Benefit and Carer's Allowance, all being paid into your bank account.

"We will be cancelling these payments and setting up a new account with Miss Jay. However, Miss Jay is adamant that you shouldn't be in receipt of any of these as you are a private medical consultant in a private establishment. We will need to investigate this fully, Mr Phoenix, as if we discover that you have claimed this fraudulently, then not only will we need all of the benefits to be paid back, but we will need to proceed with legal action; fraud of benefits is a very serious offence."

I had no words.

"So, we need a new address for you, so that we can send out paperwork and arrange to visit you."

'Think, Tom'!

"Well, obviously there has been some confusion," I replied, "I never even passed my GCSE in biology!"

Corey and Shay came in as they had heard my voice raising.

"..so I'm most definitely not a medical consultant, that's for sure!" I laughed out loud.

The boys nodded a silent greeting at me and fetched themselves a drink out of the fridge, returning to the living room. Once out of earshot, Tom continued his conversation.

"As for the address, obviously I have literally only just moved out, in fact I've not even been able pick up my stuff yet. I am, I suppose, homeless. If you give me your details, then I can contact you when I get settled."

"We do need a correspondence address for you, Mr Phoenix," the man demanded.

"Look," I replied through gritted teeth, "I have no family, I have no home, I will be living in my car for the foreseeable. I was Miss Jay's carer and those benefits were my only form of income, I'm now left with nothing, so you can't exactly do much about that!"

I hung up the phone and sat down to recover. It was partly true, the only money I had was these benefits that I received. It was true, I wasn't a consultant, and had no medical training.

The phone rang again. I just left it to ring, couldn't deal with them anymore. Good luck to them, they'd struggle to find me! I grabbed a glass from the cupboard and a bottle of scotch out of the cabinet, and poured myself two fingers. Downing it in one go, I refilled my glass. My phone continued to ring, they were very persistent. I waited until they had a break between calls and turned my phone around ready to switch it off. The calls had been from Sally.

There was no way that my life as Tom Phoenix could possibly overlap with my life as Tom Wilkins, so surely they hadn't contacted Sally; I had remained at home by her side so she'd not need to do any checks. My nerves were shattered.

I immediately rang her back.

"Are you ok, Sal?" I enquired.

"One of my clients died," she sobbed.

"Oh God, that's terrible. Are you ok?"

"No, I've called for someone to come and collect her. It looks like she took poorly over the weekend and died on her own. Her husband worked away a lot, but we can't find any details about him, or another emergency contact. I've just got to stay put until she's collected."

"Do you want me to come and sit with you for a bit?"

"That'd be great, thanks. Work has said that I can go home once it's all sorted, so could do with a lift rather than walking."

I'd had a little scotch, but if I suck a mint then she wouldn't know I was over the limit.

I grabbed my keys, "Text me the address, then I can copy

it into my maps," I suggested.

"Ok, babe, see you soon."

I rummaged through my coat pocket for my wallet and explained to the boys where I was going.

"Grim, man!" Corey exclaimed, and Shay just shrugged.

I left the house and set up my phone ready for the satnav.

Sally's text came through and I started the car.

The text was a screenshot of the client's details. 'RACHAEL SAUNDERS. 33 SWITHLAND CLOSE.'

Rachael.

Archie, Archie and Bella

<u>April 2020</u>

"It looks like it's just you and me for a while, Bella."

I sat down next to the love of my life. Just the two of us would work out fine, I was sure. Sure, we both had social lives, and sometimes followed different paths where friends were concerned, but that was ok; it doesn't always pay to be in each other's pockets.

Lockdown was new to everyone and would affect everybody. Some relationships would survive, like ours, others wouldn't. If we just agreed to stay indoors like the government insisted, then there was nothing to worry about. It was cold and wet outdoors anyway, so any excuse to not go out suited me just fine. Even the bin men wouldn't come, so we didn't need to put our bins out. Yes, staying indoors with my warm slippers and blanket would suit me just fine.

Bella looked at me, her eyes glistening slightly. "We will be fine, my love," I reassured her.

She paused for a moment, then wandered into the kitchen to get some food. Mmmmm it's like she could read my mind! I followed her in and popped the kettle on for a nice brew. Bella headed straight for the biscuits.

"Oh you cheeky minx!" I laughed. "I suppose a couple won't hurt."

Personally, I preferred chocolate digestives, and they were stored in the fridge to keep that chocolate nice and firm. "Just a couple today, eh Bella?"

I chuckled to myself as I carried the refreshments into the living room, switching the television on as I passed it. We had never really been fond of television programmes, but since we hadn't been made aware of the lockdown until a policeman stopped me in our street and told me to return home, I found that the tv gave some comfort by providing us with imperative knowledge. News was grim and depressing, but necessary it seems, and certainly better than all of these daytime shows that the young ones seem to be glued to.

Our grandson, Archie, named after me, keeps talking about 'browser' this and 'download' that; I haven't got a clue what he's talking about, God bless him. He told me to 'surf online', I checked with my local store and they decided that I must be confused, offering me 'inline skates' or surfboards; I declined, I can't do such energetic things like he can. He does make me laugh though, like when he shouts, pretending that I am deaf. If he was here right now, he'd have polished off this whole packet of biscuits! But he does love his programmes too. He's fifteen now, but still loves to come and visit us after school. I tell him that too much television will make him have square eyes, but he just laughs. He can't visit anymore, not until this lockdown is over.

May 2020

I really think I shouldn't have allowed myself two biscuits a day, as my supply is now depleted, but my waist is increasing. I suppose it is the lack of exercise. My daughter, Karen, speaks to me sometimes when Archie phones, she asks if we need anything but I decline. We don't want anyone going out of their way for us.

I used to pop into town every day and pick up some bits as and when we needed them, along with a few extra bits. 'Hoarding', Karen calls it. I bet she thinks we aren't so silly now, as we have started to break into our supplies. At first, I didn't think I'd be allowed to use them, as they are all stored in my garage. Archie assured me that we were allowed outside to some extent, and the garage would be fine. It is just other people who we aren't allowed to mingle with.

He tells me to 'shop online' by using the computer, but we only keep one here for when he stays overnight; we don't know how to use it. Bella sits and watches him when he uses it, but it's like a whole new language to her. I don't even attempt it, can't figure out how to turn the blasted thing on! He says he can do the shopping online for us, but I don't know how he can do that if he's at home. He can't come round or the policeman will arrest him.

Maybe I should consider walking around the garden like that chap on tv did recently, I could maybe lose a little of the midriff. Bella doesn't care about my weight, or hers. She's usually planted on the sofa watching her programmes. I don't care for them myself. Watching people scream at the screen, shouting out answers doesn't appeal to me in the slightest. Bella snoozes whilst watching them all the time, but if I dare to change the station with the clicker, she acts like she's watching the blessed thing! The contestants on the competition programmes are complete idiots. How can they not know if Amelia Earhart flew, sailed or drove, for goodness sake?!

<u>June 2020</u>

"FANNY, BLOODY FANNY! HOW CAN YOU NOT KNOW THAT? YOU IMBECILE!" I turned to Bella, who was looking at me strangely. "How can they NOT know that the 'Cradock' who wrote cookbooks was called Fanny? I can understand why the compere is laughing so much, it is a simple enough question, and there were 3 answers to choose from! It is obviously not Tuppence or Minnie!"

Bella simply looked away with indignation, clearly as confused as me. Her tummy rumbled, indicating that it must be lunchtime. I pressed the down button of the clicker, it said 12.55. Her hunger was early today, we had yet to watch the final round to see who wins the money, if anyone! It was rollover from yesterday as nobody knew that the cockney slang 'apples and pears' referred to 'stairs'! Time for today's final question; I pressed the up arrow on the clicker which increased the volume; I wasn't mishearing the question like I did the other day, If I had been able to hear correctly, I would have known that King Edward wasn't an Italian dictator, and the question didn't refer to any vegetables at all! Easy mistake to make, and certainly better than 'Pavarotti' and 'Linguine'.

As soon as the music came on, Bella was up like a shot and straight into the kitchen. Food certainly ruled her life, as was starting to show in her wobbly bits nowadays. I must admit though, she was exercising in the garden more than me. I only tended to potter about watering the plants these days.

Opening the cupboard door in the garage, I realised that we were now onto the tins.

"Carrots or beans, Bella?" I enquired, she just huffed indignantly and walked off. "I can defrost a couple of slices of bread in the toaster, dear, then we can have beans on toast?"

Archie had been sneaky the other week, and had dropped off some bread, butter, pasta, tuna, toilet paper and long-life milk for us, leaving it on the doorstep just before our bedtime. He had knocked on the door and shouted through the letterbox,

"Grandad, wait a minute before you answer the door."

I had no idea why he would suggest such a thing, but luckily it takes me that long to stand up and get to the door anyway. I opened it and saw the goodies on the step, with a note which read,

HERE ARE SOME BASIC FOOD ITEMS FOR YOU GRANDAD. MUM SAYS YOU MIGHT HAVE TO RATION THE BREAD SLICES, BUT I GUESS YOU'D BE USED TO THAT FROM DURING THE WAR. ARCHIE XX

During the war, cheeky bugger, I wasn't born til after it ended! Kids today, eh!

I shuffled back into the kitchen, leaving the back door open a little longer as it was a nice day, and Bella was already sunning herself in a deckchair. We'd had to resort to using the micro-oven recently, as we couldn't get our payment card topped up for the gas, so the cooker was out of action. It's lucky we have so many electrical appliances I suppose, and the beans were done in a jiffy, before the toast in fact! The butter was a little sparse, and what we did have was rather hard as we had to store it in the fridge now the warmer weather was here. Couldn't risk leaving it in the larder, didn't want it going rancid. Hard butter is better than no butter. Haha, try saying that three times fast. I was still chuckling as I took our food outside to the glass patio table that we had. The weather was indeed glorious, I could totally understand how Bella could sit out here for hours. Any warmer and I'd probably not be able to tolerate it for long. It would have been much nicer to have had salad for lunch but beans on toast would have to do.

I really shouldn't be out here for too long, Countdown is on soon!

<u>July 2020</u>

Lockdown is now over apparently. Despite thousands of people still dying, now is the time to send the children back to school for the short amount of time left before the big holidays. I had managed to get into town recently, albeit with a mask over my face. As if it wasn't warm enough already! If I didn't have to stock up my cupboards, then I wouldn't be bothering at all. Well, we did need loo roll, and I wanted to stock up a bit, as I predict the lockdown will be back on soon and wanted plenty of the basics ready, just in case.

Karen has arranged a barbeque for us this weekend, at our house as it was easier than us getting to them. Her husband, Bob was a 'dab hand' at barbeques she was telling me during one of our telephone conversations the other day. She'd bring everything, and she'd bring me another 'care package'. I won't refuse this time, you can never have too much toilet roll!

***

Karen gave me a big hug when we finally got together for the barbeque, although we had to meet in the garden, we still weren't allowed to be indoors with other family members yet. Archie gave me a 'fist hump', I believe it is called. Bob was the last in, as he wheeled through his 'kettle drum'. I was expecting a barbeque, but I guess he knows what he's doing. I approached him to proffer a handshake, he stepped back and rejected, saying we mustn't be too close as he'd only just got back to work and didn't want to jeopardise things.

"Don't forget about Bella, Karen," I reminded my daughter as she went to sit down in one of the deckchairs.

She hadn't really warmed to Bella, despite us being together for 15 years. To be quite honest, our father/daughter relationship hadn't been the same since my wife had passed away. Karen had been quite close to her mother, but I thought maybe the time we'd been forced to spend apart would have made her at least tolerate her. Then again, it seemed the feeling was mutual, as Bella strode off, disgruntled at the family gathering, flicking her tail at us as she jumped onto the wall.

Man Eats Bat?

Todd and Chris were relieved that their journey was over for now. They had enjoyed their working trip below deck on a cruise liner, but this is what they had been waiting for; backpacking across the Far East. They had arrived in China first, settling in a little city called Wuhan.

They aimed to live simply for as long as possible, although they had backup funds available back in England if they experienced any unusual circumstances. In fact, that had been the proviso for their parents allowing them to travel this far out, especially since the earthquakes and tsunamis that had hit around this time of year. It had been easier for the brothers to promise to call their parents if they experienced any difficulties than it was to explain that they weren't venturing anywhere near Indonesia. Their mum thought it was a great distance from town to home and so could not comprehend the distinction between China and another country.

Nevertheless, those were the conditions set for them if they wished to go travelling.

They found a hostel close to the centre of the city which also gave them the added assurance that their belongings would be safe too. The truth of the matter was that they didn't have the first idea about how to embark on a backpacking holiday and were a little overwhelmed from the beginning.

Upon awaking on the first day, they handed over their rucksacks to the hostel manager and headed out. They could hear the bustle of the nearby market, and their noses led them to the fine delicacies of the area. They walked slowly past each stall of weird-looking snacks, of which some bore a vague resemblance to animals. Chris turned up his nose at them, whereas Todd was more willing.

"Todd," Chris whispered to his older brother, "is it too early to regret this trip?"

Todd laughed. "Chill, bro, you'll be fine. Stick close to me."

Back home, Chris was known as a fussy eater, but it had never occurred to him that he would be faced with his biggest fear: food that looked like the animal it originated from. He even struggled with eggs, knowing that they 'came out of a chicken's bum'. When agreeing to this 'holiday', he had assumed that there would be little Chinese restaurants, like 'Oriental Garden', the all-you-can-eat which was at the end of their street, dotted all around. Even then, he targeted the plain boiled rice and crispy duck; he couldn't see either of these at the stall Todd was browsing now.

Neither of them had bothered to learn the language either, which could have resulted in a loss of communication unless Todd could rely on the translation app on his phone. At least they had brought a regional adapter plug for their phone charger lead with them!

Todd pointed to a dried out black, oddly-shaped edible item on a low table next to a fish stall. He picked one up to study the comestible closer. The old woman at the other side of the table ranted at them in her native language. Todd threw the item back down which further ignited her rage. He fumbled around in his short's pocket for his phone and shakily opened up the app, speaking into it.

"I'm sorry, I don't speak Chinese, I would like to know what this delicious treat is."

He clicked a button and held it in front of her. It repeated what he had said in, he hoped, a language that she would understand.

She picked up the delicacy 'treat' with her grubby fingers and held out her other hand for money, refusing to speak back into the phone. Todd shakily rifled through another pocket and found a note of unknown value. He offered it to the woman who gladly accepted it and handed over the odd item. They loitered a little longer, hoping for some change but she waved them away.

They nervously moved along to the next stand, which had dozens of dead chickens, de-feathered. This was a no-go for Chris, of course! The next, live chickens was even worse. There was an alleyway next to the feathered fowl and they ducked in.

"We are so in over our heads, man!" Chris stated nervously.

"Shhhh," Todd replied, "we just need to find our feet a bit."

They both stood next to a wall and inspected Todd's purchase.

"It looks like, a bat?" Chris suggested.

"A bat? I thought it was a frog," Todd admitted.

"A frog??" Chris repeated. "There's toads that are used as drugs but are also poisonous enough to kill you. Don't eat it!"

"That's BS, mate, just a nibble won't hurt." He sniffed it and recoiled. "Hmmm, maybe I'll just stick it in my bag..... oh, that's back at the hostel. Ok, so, in for a dollar....."

He bit into it, and it crunched. He scrunched up his nose as he chewed what seemed like rubber.

"What are you doing?!" Chris exclaimed incredulously.

"Attempting to eat the bat," Todd replied, grinning.

"What if you are meant to cook it first? You don't even know what it is!"

Chris opened a new browser on his smartphone and started searching for images of edible bats or frogs but failed to find anything. He looked up from his phone to find his brother munching more of it.

"Stop, Todd, you've made your point!"

Todd threw the remainder of the snack into a nearby bin, his eyes twinkling with mischief. He liked to tease his brother but knew where to draw the line.

"C'mon, let's go and find something better to eat!"

They found a little eatery a few streets away, and Chris was relieved to find ribs and prawn crackers, and plain rice of course.

Sated, they decided it was time to start having fun. They spotted an orange light flickering above a doorway which led to a flight of wooden stairs. Music could be faintly heard, and they spotted a couple of young locals ascending the stairs as they approached the doorway, so they chose to follow them.

The bar, they assumed it was a bar, was dark and dingy. If Wuhan had educational establishments, which the brothers weren't sure about, then this could be considered a student night, as the place was heaving with adolescents. Like student nights back home, to which they had attended a few, you could feel the beat of the music underfoot.

They found a small area against a back wall that wasn't occupied to stand by, and Todd ventured towards the bar to get some drinks. Finding a wall of spirits in front of him he breathed a sigh of relief. 'Finally, something I recognise!'. He ordered two JDs with coke and walk-danced back to Chris. No sooner had he returned than they were approached by two young women.

The brothers had formulated a secret code back in England; a glance which indicated that they should be aware of possible scams or threats, and Todd raised his eyebrows to alert Chris, who gave a faint nod back at him to show his acknowledgement.

The young men had already put some security measures into place; passports were stuffed down pants, phones and loose change and one small value note in front pockets and other monetary notes were in shoes. When one note was spent, it would be discreetly replaced.

More girls flocked around the young English patrons, like they were the rock stars. They had the choice of the pack, it seemed. Chris took quite a shine to the one with the long black hair and gothic makeup. Todd preferred the one with the short black hair and equally dark makeup. They clearly had the same taste in women.

Once the others realised that they couldn't win the brothers' attention they dispersed, hunting for someone else. This was a weekly ritual for these ladies; to look for a mate, preferably exotic. The two youths from the north of England were far from exotic but these women were only interested in a release, whether it be a new lifestyle or just a quick relief from their own lives.

They danced and drank and kissed in the shadows. Todd's girl tried to 'get down' right there in the club whereas Chris' had more patience. They staggered back to their hostel but were refused entry; the girls weren't allowed. Equally, the girls didn't seem to have an alternative place to go, so the boys kissed goodbye to their short-term friends outside the residence. The ladies didn't give in easily though and tried to entice them with love bites and offers of doorway liaisons. Todd submitted and disappeared down an alleyway. Chris bid his companion goodbye and returned to the hostel.

He lay on the uncomfortable camp bed staring at the ceiling for what seemed like hours, but Todd never returned. He text his brother several times, asking when he would be back but there was no response. Eventually he drifted into a fretful sleep, more like being awake with his eyes shut. He was prone to worry at the best of times, and this was unfamiliar territory.

The following morning Chris was at a loss about what to do next. He had attempted to call his backpacking companion, but he still couldn't get through to him. He decided to leave a note at the hostel for Todd to contact him and collected all of their belongings from the manager at the same time. During his semi-conscious night, he had decided that they should return home. Chris was in too deep and Todd had already broken their pact to stay together. He knew that his sibling had possession of his vital personal items and was competent enough to stay the course. It was time for him to use one of his lifelines, their parents.

"Hi, Mum, it's Chris."

"Ohh, Christopher, what's the matter, dear, it's 2 a.m.!"

Crap! He'd completely forgotten about the time difference. He was hoping to speak to his father, as his mother had the same worrying traits that had caused Chris to make this monumental decision in the first place.

"N…No, there's nothing wrong, didn't realise about the time difference, sorry, Mum."

"Oh, ok, Son. Is your brother there?"

"Erm…. No, he's just nipped into a shop, I'll get him to call you later. Is Dad there?"

"I think he's still downstairs, I'll pop and check."

"Thanks, Mum. Sorry I woke you."

"That's ok, darling. Here's your father now."

Chris could hear his dad clear his throat, as he always did before speaking on the phone.

"Yes, Chris, how are you both? Having fun?"

"Yeeahh, Dad. Well, no, but don't say anything to Mum. I'm really not digging this place, Dad, and I think we need to come home early."

"Oh, Christopher, that's not good. Where are you?"

"We're in Wuhan."

"Right, right. So, ahem, when were you thinking of coming home?"

"As soon as possible, Dad."

"Right, that doesn't sound good. Wasn't Wuhan the first place on the trip?"

"Yes. Look, Dad, I don't have much battery life on my phone or credit. Can you help us sort flights please?"

"Right, right I see. Ok, ahem, well if you both make your way to the airport, there will be places that you can charge your phones. Do you have money to get there and rent a charging station, or whatever it is called?"

"Yes,"

"Right, right. Well you boys do that and then I will sort out flights and call you back in a couple of hours."

"Thanks, Dad," Chris breathed a sigh of relief.

"Right, yes, so sort that out then."

His father ended the phone call and Chris first headed to the entrance of the club they had visited the previous night, on the off chance that Todd would be there. He wasn't. He sombrely walked to the nearest taxi rank and caught a ride to the airport.

Luckily he found a charging station for his phone, and perched himself on the stool just inside the entrance at the airport. His father rang right on schedule.

"I tried to ring your brother, but his phone was switched off," he announced.

"Yes, erm… we were both short on battery life so he offered to let me use the charger first, as it was my phone you said you would ring."

'Good thinking, Chris!' he thought to himself.

"Right, right, ahem," he cleared his throat. "I have booked you both onto the next flight home, but it isn't until tomorrow at 4.30 a.m. I will send you the, erm, ahem, electronic tickets, to your phone, Christopher?"

"Yes please, Dad. Thank you so, so much!" Chris beamed, relief written all over his face.

He knew that this gave the brothers some time to reunite, hopefully.

"Yes, yes, ahem, I've booked you both into a hotel next to the airport for tonight, but obviously set yourself an alarm to make sure you don't miss your flight."

"Oh, Dad, you are the best."

"Right, yes. Just tell the concierge your name and she, well they, as it could be a man I suppose, they can let you into your room."

"Concierge?"

"Yes, Christopher. The reception desk person. They are usually multi-lingual. They will help you."

He gave his youngest son the details of the hotel and ended the call.

Chris looked round for some kind of contact point and found a sign with an 'i' above a small desk. He managed to leave a detailed, anxious written message with the person on duty, a friendly older lady, for Todd to receive upon entering the airport.

Taking a deep breath, he looked around for directions to the hotel. Once there, the receptionist dealt with his check-in quickly and he was soon flat out on a very comfortable bed.

Chris was rudely awoken several hours later by the sound of retching in the bathroom. He panicked and sat up abruptly, seeing his big brother exit the en suite, wiping his mouth.

"Todd!" he gasped, jumping up to hug him.

"Hey," Todd backed away, "Don't come too close, I've got some kind of bug. Don't know if it is catching or if it's that dodgy frog thing I ate yesterday." He dry-heaved at the mere thought of it.

"Or the extreme amounts of alcohol you consumed last night?" Chris suggested, as Todd swiftly returned to the bathroom.

He returned to the room a few minutes later, looking very pasty and clammy. He collapsed on the bed and was asleep in seconds.

The journey home was turbulent and very long. Todd had now stopped vomiting but was very weak and dehydrated. He slept for most of the flight, only rousing for water.

Their father was waiting at the airport when they landed and whisked them home without question. They all crept into the house silently and headed straight to bed.

***

The next morning Todd was up with the lark, 'bright and breezy', making a fry up for the whole family. Their mum squealed with delight, realising that her boys were safe and sound.

"I never wanted you both to go there in the first place," she explained, not for the first time this year.

"Well we are home safe now," Todd replied, kissing her on the cheek and squeezing her tight.

Chris entered the room, feeling jetlagged and lightheaded.

"Think I've got what you had, Bro!"

"Naa, mate," Todd replied, "No-one can be as bad as I was!" Todd laughed.

"Well, I didn't eat a bat, to be fair," Chris joked.

"A bat, Todd?" Mother swung round to confront him.

"Naa, Mam, it was just a bit of a frog!"

"A BIT OF A FROG?!"

Todd laughed and plated up the breakfast items. "You want me to eat yours, Chris?" he asked.

"Nope, I feel like crap, but could still eat a horse!"

"YOU ATE A HORSE TOO?!"

As they all tucked into their food, their dad leaned over to Todd. "Is that a tattoo you have on your neck, Son?" he asked, touching a raw area of skin on the young man's neck.

Todd flinched. "Naa, mosquitoes," he replied, pulling his collar up to cover it up.

"You can catch malaria out there, can't you?" their mum joined the conversation.

"I've not got malaria, Mum," Todd stated.

She turned round to look at Chris. "What about you, Christopher?"

"What about me?" Chris replied.

"Malaria?"

"No, Mum, it's just the change of climate, like a cold or something."

Once everyone had finished, their mum cleared away the pots and made a start on the washing up. The boys went back upstairs to their bedroom.

"So?" Chris probed, once out of earshot.

"So, what?" Todd replied.

"What the hell happened?"

"I have no idea. I remember us being outside the hostel, and that bird enticed me into an alleyway. I woke up the next day in a local park."

"A park?"

Todd nodded. "You know you've got a mark on your neck like mine," he mentioned casually.

Chris' hand shot straight up to feel it and stood up to look in their mirror on the wardrobe door. Sure enough, he discovered two small puncture holes, and a very slight black vine shape branching away from it.

"You know it was daylight by the time we split up that night?"

"What?" Chris replied. "How?"

He thought back to that night, and yes, it was just getting light when he had returned to the hostel.

"It's like we lost a few hours of our lives?"

They looked at each other blankly.

***

For the following few weeks, the boys noticed some changes as they returned to their normal lives. Todd's hair darkened to the same shade as his brother's. Their senses were heightened to incredible levels. Their eyes darkened and their skin lightened. This was all very subtle to them and was only noticed by the friends that they hadn't seen since they returned from their trip.

They seemed to have developed a kind of animal magnetism too. Women veered towards them at all opportunities, sometimes in droves. They oozed charisma without even trying. Todd chose to play the field, having a different girlfriend every night of the week. Todd was more timid, despite the hordes of girls being quite insistent. He resisted their advances for as long as possible, but eventually surrendered.

At first they covered up their neck abrasions, but soon they embraced them as they became more visible and intricate. Friends, new and old, were drawn to them too, wanting to know where they got their tattoos. They slept during the day and partied all night. Every night they were out in various clubs with a different girl on their arm. Different groups of friends were buying them drinks all night and they wouldn't get home until the early hours of the morning. Similarly to China, they were also losing time, usually around the hours of 2-4 a.m.

Their friends were having similar experiences; neck marks, lost hours, seductiveness. Nightclubs were abundant with devotees and a trend seemed to be forming for complex neck tattoos.

But soon, things took a sinister turn. Relatives of these youths started falling ill, some even dying. Todd and Chris started having vivid dreams and sometimes even night terrors, which were more like flashbacks or foreshadowing.

Across the UK were thousands of deaths, overwhelming the emergency services' resources. Bodies were being stockpiled in hospital wards following a ban on funerals. The public were advised, no, instructed to stay indoors.

The ever-increasing group of seemingly invincible youths chose to ignore this, even their own relatives' deaths not deterring them. Clubs, restaurants and other social gathering places were forced to close, so the youths convened in other locations.

This new strain of human, because let's face it, that's what they had become, met up in barns, empty houses, derelict buildings, and just sat in the dark. Gatherers had formed; groups of youths who collected recently deceased humans and brought them to the larger groups. They assembled in colonies and feasted on the departed mortals.

They continued to inhabit dark and damp constructions.

The news reports stated that the cause of this, this 'virus' had been rumoured to have been one sole man eating a bat, in Wuhan, China.

Todd reflected back to his night in Wuhan. One girl had been the source of his punctured skin. A vampire, maybe? A vampire bat??

The truth was that one 'bat' had 'eaten' one man.

Shipshape and Bristol Fashion

"Can't you just feel the bracing cold air, Phil? The sky is quite clear tonight too, so we should see the aurora borealis later on."

"I can't wait, dear, but let's go and eat first," Phoebe's husband replied.

Phil would have preferred a cruise to the warmer parts of the world this winter, but as Phoebe had paid, she held all the trump cards. Luckily, she had packed plenty of woolly jumpers for him.

They went back to their room to change for dinner; it was formal dress every evening. Wearing a gold sequined dress, Phoebe shimmered as she glided into the dining hall. Phil stayed the course with his black suit, along with a blue shirt and paisley tie, all chosen by his attentive wife. They took their seats at the table allocated to them for the duration of the Nordic cruise, greeting their new companions, Wyatt and Simon.

The subject of the all-male couple was skirted over at the beginning of the trip, Phoebe preferring not to be forced to consider this relationship as a valid option. There had been a couple of slip-ups earlier on in their journey, but they all knew it wasn't malicious; they had to endure each other for 99 nights, so there was no point getting upset and angry.

Several other subjects were avoided alongside homosexuality, or indeed any relationships that were considered 'abnormal'. Phoebe wasn't phobic of any diversity, she just spoke before she thought and had no filter. The bypassed conversations included children and religion; Phoebe was from a long line of devout Christians and was always the first at the ship's chapel every Sunday morning, whereas Wyatt and Simon were non-denominational, possibly even heathens. Although Phil had advised that she shouldn't say grace, she insisted that this was essential. Being thankful that God (or Jesus) guided the chef to make the delicious food, that He had encouraged the buyers of the food to choose those ingredients to provide the meal, or had grown the vegetables and created edible animals, that they were lucky enough to be on this cruise ship to experience this incredible dish.

Today's starter was a fish soup, and Phoebe knew the etiquette for eating/drinking soup, but preferred to study then three men at her table to ensure that they didn't slurp or put the whole soup spoon in their mouth. Phil knew better than to do that, but would the others have the knowledge and elegance to follow suit? The men chose neither and tucked into the delicious freshly baked bread, dunking it into the steaming liquid in their bowls.

Phil leaned over to his wife and whispered, "Just ignore them, dear, it really doesn't matter."

"If only it was that simple," was her exasperated reply.

"Please don't make a scene, Phee," he pleaded. "Look, they are preparing the stage for tonight's act. I believe it is a singer local to the area...."

"I think I'm going to go and have a lie down, sweetheart," Simon announced to his partner.

"I will come with you," Wyatt offered.

"Can they not just wait until after dinner," Phoebe muttered to her husband, louder than Phil had hoped.

"Shhh, dear," he replied, while smiling at the young couple apologetically.

"There's a time and a place, Phil, that's all I'm saying."

She really didn't need to elaborate.

"No, thank you, Wy," Simon replied, ignoring the comments of their table buddy. "I'm just feeling a little under the weather, hun."

Phoebe flinched at the pet names but refrained from further verbal opinions. Simon politely excused himself, kissing Wyatt as he left.

The starter crockery and cutlery was cleared away by very efficient waiting staff, and the main was served in no time. Reindeer with dauphinoise potatoes and green beans, served with a red wine jus.

"I guess Santa got fed up of Rudolph," they heard a voice from another table.

Phoebe flinched and her eye twitched. "Cutbacks, eh Chantelle, coz of Brexit."

Phoebe wanted to turn round and explain to them just how many errors were in that short conversation. Luckily, the pianist started playing Chopin and that calmed her down.

They ate their main course in silence, Phoebe preferring

to listen to the music without being disturbed.

Dessert was a choice of a deconstructed cheesecake, which Wyatt had chosen, cheese and biscuits, which was Phoebe's preference, and Irish coffee, which was Phil's indulgence. Wyatt ate his cheesecake in record time, and had arranged for Simon to have cheese and biscuits to go, which the waiter brought in a very fancy embellished box. He made his excuses and left to tend to his unwell companion.

The older couple stayed until around 9 p.m., then left the dining hall, taking the long way back to their room to avoid passing the room of the young men they shared mealtimes with, in case they were 'partaking in any unsolicited activities'.

Due to all of the unexpected events of the evening, both forgot to observe the northern lights.

***

Phoebe rose early the next morning, as she did every day, and headed for the pool where she enjoyed her exercise ritual. As she arrived, she noticed that no staff were available to greet her. Unperturbed, she continued to get changed in the restrooms, entered the pool and commenced her lengths. The warmth of the water was a welcome contrast to the bitter air she had briefly experienced during her short journey to the leisure facility.

Satisfied with her desired performance, she returned to the changing rooms and showered. As she exited the building, she was greeted by the duty lifeguard, who was removing excess water from the poolside.

'I assume it was a shift change', Phoebe thought to herself as she meandered back to her room, the long way again. Once back in her room, she woke Phil up so that they could get ready for breakfast.

Face fully made up ready for the day ahead, the married couple entered the dining hall for breakfast. The room wasn't particularly full, but Phoebe preferred it this way. Phil always ordered the full English (he wasn't good with 'foreign food') and Phoebe enjoyed a selection including grapefruit, Eggs Benedict and plenty of coffee.

"Mmm, the hollandaise sauce is impeccable today, dear," Phoebe exclaimed, elegantly of course.

Her tone indicated that the statement was rhetorical, as Phil had a mouthful of black pudding. He had taken a few years to be eloquent enough to meet his wife's standards, but she had trained him well.

"What do you have planned for the day?" she asked him, this time requiring a response.

"Bowls!" he replied.

She glared at his impertinence.

"Do you mean lawn bowling, Phil?" she corrected.

Phil nodded, considering himself told.

As they left breakfast, they went their separate ways, as Phoebe was booked in for a massage.

She sat patiently in the waiting area, checking her gold watch every minute or so, tutting to herself. The receptionist shifted nervously, and occasionally rang a supervisor for advice. Eventually, the manager appeared in the waiting area and approached Phoebe, her high heels clicking on the immaculately white tiled floor.

"Mrs...." she glanced at her clipboard, "Barrington-Smythe. My name is Leanne and I am the general manager of the leisure facilities. Unfortunately, we are a little under-staffed today, madam."

Phoebe Barrington-Smythe could feel her blood pressure rising.

"Ms...?" she probed, wanting to remain formal for this interaction.

"Cartwright," the manager responded, "Leanne Cartwright."

"Ms Cartwright, what is the solution to this issue?"

There was small silence.

"We are going to have cancel today's...." she glanced at her clipboard again, "massage," she concluded prematurely.

The two women looked blankly at each other; one searching for answers and one hoping for a peaceful resolution.

"Well, when can you rebook this for me? This afternoon?"

"Today won't be possible," the member of the crew responded, hoping this would suffice.

"Well tomorrow then?" Phoebe insisted.

"You can certainly drop by and see what the situation is then?" Leanne Cartwright suggested.

"Drop by," Phoebe scoffed. "Just, like, on the off-chance?" The manager nodded. "This is not acceptable!"

Leanne nervously replied, "We are happy to offer you complimentary...."

"Complimentary what, exactly? It is all-inclusive cruise. I could have several massages a day if I so choose, so what can you offer me?"

Leanne desperate searched for an adequate response. She rummaged in her jacket pocket and produced a black velvet pouch, which she had been pre-authorised to use if the situation became dire.

"I would like to offer you this," she said tentatively, handing over the pouch, which was tastefully embellished with the logo of the cruise company, with plaited cord in corporate colours of gold and black. "It is £200 worth of casino chips which can be used at any of our casino nights."

Phoebe was suitable impressed and accepted the gesture of goodwill. Leanne escorted the guest out of the facilities and returned to the receptionist.

"You may as well go home for the day, Ffion. Contact all of the guests booked in for today and apologise. Try not to offer such an expensive 'gesture of goodwill' though. There's a list of offers in the training manual. Go through it point by point, judge the reaction before it happens. Then lock up and go back to your room."

Ffion agreed and Leanne vacated the facility.

Phoebe returned to her stateroom to consult the cruise guide and find something to occupy her mind.

Pool: done.

Therapies: unavailable.

Salon: no point as the hairstyle will be ruined by swimming in the morning.

Lawn Sports: Phil was already enjoying today's activity of lawn bowls.

The only options left were a brisk walk along the deck, or to remain in the room and watch tv or listen to the radio. She chose the latter, keeping the volume low on the radio so that she could read to herself. She had recently learned to speak Mandarin following her retirement last year, and had picked up a couple of books of short stories, written in Chinese, when they stopped off in Hong Kong a few weeks ago, so set about assessing how quickly she could translate the text.

Forty-five minutes into the solitude of their room, there was a knock at the door. Upon answering, Phoebe was faced with a youth in corporate uniform.

"Hello, Mrs Barrington-Smythe, I am Barney. We are offering a room service lunch today and I have been sent to provide you with the menu choices. Someone will phone you at 11 a.m., to discuss your choices." Barney handed her the menu and smiled politely, before leaving Phoebe standing at the door, holding the laminated menu.

She was still standing at the open door when Phil returned from his bowling session. Phoebe repeated the events of the day so far and handed her husband the laminated menu. Known for taking everything in his stride, he studied the menu for a few minutes, then handed it back to his irate wife, who had been ranting about the poor service the whole time.

The phone rang as Phoebe was still pacing the floor, ready to complain. Phil answered the call before his wife could get to it and confirmed his lunchtime selection. He turned to his wife and enquired about her choice.

"WHATEVER!" she replied, with hostility that was colder than the deck of the ship.

"Make that two of everything," he informed the caller.

Half an hour later, a smorgasbord of cold meats, bread and cheese arrived, along with a bottle of complimentary champagne and a fresh fruit platter. After lunch they both had a much-needed nap.

When they awoke, it was almost time for dinner. They took turns in the bathroom, Phoebe having the first turn as she had more to do once out of the shower. Tonight, she chose a black silk long-length dress and a black faux fur stole. With the assistance of his wife, Phil dressed in a jumper rather than jacket, so that they could witness the aurora display after dinner.

There was no sign of either of the lovers at the Barrington-Smythe's table during dinner service. Phoebe enquired with one of the waiting staff, who reached into their shirt pocket and produced a list of passengers.

"Wyatt Sargant and Simon Stornaway-Sargant are a little under the weather," she informed them, and then left with the dirty pots she had cleared from their table.

Just before dessert, the captain appeared on stage.

"Hello, ladies and gentlemen. Our scheduled act for tonight, Paula White, is not able to join us." There were several groans and mutterings amongst the holidaymakers. "However," she continued, "We do have a fantastic evening of poker, roulette and blackjack prepared for you, along with complimentary cocktails, just over in the Executive Lounge."

A whoop erupted from the table with the Texans on, making Phoebe's neck hairs raise of their own accord.

"Surely they should have checked the quality of the guests before accepting their money, knowing that we all have to share the same space for 99 nights!" Phoebe whispered to her husband.

The casino night proved to be a success, especially when Phil managed to clear the Texans' chips in one game of blackjack. Lincoln, the male of the family made a threat of getting them back next time, in the annoying Texan drawl that grated Phoebe so easily.

The Barrington-Smythe couple managed to trade in one of their £100 casino chips for a bottle of champagne and the pair staggered back to their cabin, more than slightly inebriated. They sat in the chairs outside their room and quietly celebrated their success under the northern light show.

As they stood up to return to their cabin, they came upon

Wyatt, who was nervously smoking a cigarette by his front door. The couple nodded to him and politely asked after his companion.

"He died last night," came the unexpected reply.

The older couple were dumbstruck. Phil placed a comforting hand on his arm, which made his wife gasp.

"Don't touch him, or you could catch AIDS!" she exclaimed.

It was Wyatt's turn to gasp this time. "He had an asthma attack!" he snapped back at her, returning to his room and slamming the door.

"What on earth, Phee?" Phil questioned his wife once back in their stateroom.

"Gays catch AIDS, Phil, it's a fact!"

Phil was speechless and walked away from her. He disappeared into their bathroom and returned wearing his pyjamas a few minutes later. He climbed into bed and turned away from his wife. Phoebe sat by the desk and poured some champagne into one of their glasses. After finishing the whole bottle she fell asleep, still fully clothed.

***

The next morning, they both awoke with a headache. Phoebe skipped her daily swim and chose several cups of coffee instead. Once they had enough caffeine in their system, they ventured to the dining hall for breakfast. As they passed the Stornaway-Sargant's room they heard Wyatt coughing.

"Smoker's cough," Phoebe commented.

Phil bit his tongue, refusing to argue with his wife so early in the morning. They entered the hall in silence and headed straight for their regular table. There appeared to be buzz of excitement in the air, as the excursion to Oslo was planned for immediately after breakfast.

Phoebe, usually a very organised person, had completely forgotten and instead was dressed in more formal attire. They both would have to return to their cabin to dress more casually and warmer, before the excursion began. She stopped a young man who was dressed in smart corporate colours to inform him of her plans, so that they didn't leave the couple behind. She had planned many activities once on shore. The young man, whose name badge indicated that his name was Colin, informed them that the excursion had been postponed.

"POSTPONED?" Phoebe shrilled, a lot louder than Colin had hoped.

The reaction reverberated around the half-empty hall, causing a ruckus amongst the remaining guests. Holidaymakers were demanding more information, they deserved the truth, they exclaimed. All refused to leave until eventually the captain appeared on the same stage where she had stood last night.

"Please, can we have some order please," she shouted over the many demands, holding up her hands.

A member of the crew passed her a microphone; she meant business. She dragged over a stool from the edge of the platform and sat on it.

"Ok, people. It's true, we have been forced to cancel our excursion for today." She hushed away the murmurs. "Oslo is a wonderful city, and it pains us not to be able to go too, but this is bigger than just us. Since we set sail a few weeks ago, there has been trouble on land. A global pandemic has hit, and is, in a nutshell, spreading like wildfire.

"All ports around most of the world are now closed. We are planning to dock at Oslo as planned, but only to refuel. We will then continue our journey and play it by ear.

"We haven't any idea about the length of time we will have to remain on the ship, but we have been officially placed in quarantine following several deaths on board. Now, don't panic though, only those with weak immune systems have died, and their bodies are safe and secure in part of the ship's infirmary.

"Not a lot of information is available to us yet, not available to us as a whole global population. This includes not knowing how the virus," she looked at her notes, "Corona, they are calling it, spreads. From now on, everyone must stay in their cabins until advised otherwise. We have added BBC News 24 to your tv channels, and you will all be able to monitor the situation as it is broadcast to those on land.

"When we stock up on fuel, we will also collect food supplies, which will be completely sealed and labelled according to dietary requirements. Our waiting staff are going to be handing out some forms for you all to complete. Although this is a luxury liner, supplies are going to be greatly limited. This is not ideal but needs must."

The whole of the dining hall was silent as they all processed the information.

The captain continued after a short pause. "All sorts of information needs to be processed through your minds. The last thing we need is a state of panic, as this won't achieve anything."

An older man approached the captain on the stage. "This here is Dr Patel. He is one of our onboard doctors." She gestured to the doctor, who stood a short distance away from her.

"Hello, everyone. What we know at present is that the virus seems to affect the respiratory system. Anyone who suffers from any ailments that affect your breathing, such as severe asthma or COPD, please stay behind after this meeting and I will discuss any further action that you need to take."

A few of the passengers stayed behind to chat to the duty physician; Phil and Phoebe returned to their stateroom as advised.

"Surely we can still walk along the deck?" Phoebe exclaimed to her husband.

"Let's just wait and see what the captain says first, dear."

"It's preposterous! We are being treated like prisoners!"

"I think that's what the whole world is thinking right now, it isn't just us."

On a normal day, Phoebe would be quite contented to sit

in her room, watch tv, listen to the radio, do the newspaper crossword, play cards or read. All of those options were readily available to her, but instead she chose to pace the room like a caged tiger. She sighed and huffed and tutted regularly, peering out of the tiny window.

The day passed slowly, and the day after, and the day after that too. Any passenger on a normal cruise would love for the days to seem prolonged, but without leisure facilities there wasn't much they could do to make this journey a pleasant one. It would certainly be memorable though!

Unopened packets of foods were distributed amongst the guests; biscuits, cheeses, fruits, bread rolls and conserves.

On the fourth day they docked at Oslo, to refuel and obtain more food supplies. Having not been out of their room for such a long time, Phoebe ventured out of the door while Phil was taking a long and leisurely bath. There was a member of the ship's staff, Barney, standing outside in the bitterly cold wind, to ensure that nobody strayed, which was Phoebe's plan.

"Please, madam, return to your room," he insisted.

She could see other crew members loading up the food supplies in the distance.

"*They* are allowed to enter Norway, why can't I?" she gestured toward the other staff members. "It's on my bucket list, you know."

"I understand, madam, but it's out of my hands."

She took a couple more steps along the deck. What could this young whippersnapper do to stop her?

"Madam," he called louder, retrieving his walkie talkie from his pocket, ready to contact someone more senior.

"Look," she smiled sweetly, "how can I persuade you to allow me to just have a little trip on land?"

She pulled a £50 note out of her trouser pocket, attempting to discreetly hand it to the guard.

"Madam!" he exclaimed, stepping further away from her, "at present, it is against the law to enter any country. All countries are locked down, no entry or exit, for risk of spreading this virus."

She fished another £50 note out of her other pocket. Leanne Cartwright, the leisure supervisor appeared, wearing a large clear plastic visor over her face. She ushered her adversary back into her cabin.

"If you don't abide by the rules, I have the authority to lock you in, madam," she threatened.

As she was forcefully placed into her room, Phil appeared from the bathroom, naked. He stood and glared at the ship's employee before grabbing a pillow to hide his private parts.

"Phil!" Phoebe squealed, almost hysterically.

"Sir," the young lady shrieked, in shock and embarrassment.

Ms Cartwright closed the door and could be heard giggling to Barney, explaining what had happened.

Phoebe crumpled onto the bed, sobbing.

"The humiliation!" she cried.

"Well what do you expect, attempting to get off the ship?" he replied, shaking his head and removing the pillow from his groin area.

"Not me, YOU!" she whispered furiously.

Phil always knew when his wife was truly cross, and knew that the quieter her voice got, the angrier she was.

But Phil wasn't best pleased himself. "How dare you *illegally* attempt to bribe your way out of a situation?!"

"Money can get you anything you could possibly desire, Phil."

"Well clearly it can't!" he retorted through gritted teeth, storming back into the bathroom.

Phoebe lay on the bed and gently cried herself to sleep.

Both Barrington-Smythes were woken from their slumber by a knock at the door. Phoebe refused to answer it, her humiliation still stinging. Phil reluctantly opened the door to find a large care package on the doorstep. He dragged it into their room with great gusto; it was too heavy to lift. As he opened the box, he found a sealed envelope. He opened it to find a letter from the captain. He opened it and started to read it out loud.

"To our valued guests…," he began.

Phoebe snorted. "They can't even bother to learn our names," she scoffed.

"Phee! Do you have any idea how much the captain has on her plate right now?"

She shrugged and started unloading the boxes while Phil resumed reading the note.

"I hope you are well. These are unprecedented circumstances, and we are working as hard as possible to make this situation comfortable for all aboard. Celebration Cruises Plc have created this care package for our guests, and inside you will find the following:"

Phil paused as he noticed that his wife was removing everything from the box. "Get a pen, Phil, so we can make sure they have included everything that they have stated."

Shaking his head, he reached over to the desk and retrieved a pencil from the drawer.

"Thirty individually wrapped brioche buns."

"Check."

"A variety of small conserve jars."

"Check. That's all we need, more bloody jam!" Her husband chose to ignore her snide comments.

Towels, with a laundry bag to secure old towels which needed washing, to be left outside the door every Monday morning.

"We have to use the same towels for a week?!"

Toilet roll. More fruit, biscuits, crackers and cheese. Tea, coffee, sugar, mini cartons of milk. Tinned meats and fish. Disposable gloves and face masks.

'Every day, our guests will be allowed an hour a day in which they are free to walk around the deck for some fresh air. There will also be an allocated time for dinner. Within this package you will find a rota for the exercise and mealtime routines, to avoid as much contact with other guests as possible.'

"Does it say anything about the pool, dear?" Phoebe enquired.

"No," her husband replied, "I guess until they know how the virus is caught, they can't allow that sort of thing."

"What about the salon? And the spa treatments?"

Phil looked at her with a blank expression; was she really being serious? He shook his head in disbelief.

An hour for walking around the deck turned out to be as tedious as staying in their room all day, but Phoebe was determined to get her money's worth. If they allowed an hour, she would bloody well take an hour. Not a minute less. The dining hall was sectioned off with only half the usual tables in there, and they were only allowed to sit within their 'cabin families'.

Phil noticed Wyatt in the hall at the same time one day. Clearly grief-ridden, he simply pushed his food around the plate until it was time to go.

The chef had cleverly renamed the menu 'Nouvelle Cuisine', due to its smaller portions, to allow for the rations they had been given to use.

There was still plenty of alcohol left, and the waiting staff had been instructed to be a little more generous with their servings, as a gesture of good will, as well as to warm up the guests and 'relax them a little'.

The days dragged by, but the food portions became larger; this was due to there being less mouths to feed. The on-board infirmary was jam-packed with bodies, and the crew had started to use recently vacated cabins to store more. They were lucky that they were on the Nordic cruise, because if it had been a warmer climate, the smell would have become more overwhelming, not to mention the flies they would attract!

After a couple of weeks, the chef and the captain had passed away. Without a leader, a mutiny was inevitable. Not surprisingly, Phoebe took charge, and began directing all guests to play their part. Some cooked for the other passengers, some cleaned the leisure areas so that the remaining guests could use the pool, sauna and steam room. Phoebe, of course, ensured that there was nothing too strenuous for her to do. She decided that her role would be best served within the leisure facilities, supervising guests.

The numbers dwindled over the course of the next few weeks. The remaining crew members continued to collect food, but fuel was no longer required as acting captain, Phoebe, decided they should moor at the nearest port. Of course, nobody knew which port it was, as nobody spoke the language.

Every day there was a time for prayer at the ship's chapel. The interdenominational preacher had long gone, but Phoebe's faith was strong enough to embrace that role. Her mission was to convert all of the remaining passengers. They all prayed for a cure, for their souls to be saved. Prayed for loved ones who had succumbed to the virus.

A couple of guests chose to take their own lives; they considered this to be better than the horrific way other guests had suffered once infected.

Eventually, Phoebe and Phil were struck down permanently; not through the virus, but through hypothermia, as the remaining crew didn't know how to maintain the basic utilities of the ship. By the time authorities were able to assist them, all souls on board perished, the last of whom weren't the rich, but the crew who had worked the hardest for the least reward.

Glitter

"Did we all have a good time at home, children?" I enthusiastically asked the class of 31 children that, the truth be told, I had missed for the last few months.

"Yeeaahhh!" they all replied enthusiastically.

"But surely you are glad to be back?" I beamed.

Funnily enough, not every child responded quite as enthusiastically this time.

"I bet you have all missed your friends, and being able to play out?"

"Yeaahhh!" they shouted happily, a few standing up to hug their friends.

"Now, children, you know you are not allowed to hug each other. Do you remember what you were told in assembly?"

Assembly was now held with small batches of children who sat apart; the two-metre rule seemed to be out of the window right now though. Mutterings and moans of the youngsters echoed my own, although at least I was able to understand the gravity of the situation. How on earth were you meant to explain to 5-year-olds that being too close could inadvertently kill someone?

'Oooh, watch out, don't forget that kids can't be left unattended for such thoughts!' I thought to myself as I turned my attention back to the rowdy bunch.

"OK, settle down!" I shouted, hoping to claw back some kind of control.

I had been advised to interrogate, oops erm sorry, discuss with each individual child what their parents had taught them during their home-schooling experience of the last few months. Clearly this was decided by a 'suit' who had no idea about children of this age. Instead, I chose for them to create a picture of them spending time with their families; focus on the positives of this wretched situation. That way, I could chat to them about their pictures, was the way I thought of it.

The art and craft activities were handed out to each table, courtesy of the teacher's pets, or rather 'art monitors' as I was to call them. This week, it was the turn of Ella, Grace and Cerise.

The latter had chosen from an early age to dislike the colour pink with a passion, much to her mother's dismay. Whether said mother had chosen to smother her in pink as a baby, as the name implied, I was unsure, but she had even been known to screech when given anything pink to wear, eat, drink or hold. Apart from that, I quite liked her; she was quite forthright but caring at the same time and would embrace the important role of 'art monitor'.

Grace was a glitter girl. Everything she wanted had to be glitter. Glitter shoes, socks, headbands... and yes, pink mainly. Luckily, she didn't sit too near Cerise, and I had despatched them to opposite ends of the classroom.

Ella was a glue fiend. She'd smother her hands in the pva if not properly supervised, peeling it off when dry, like sunburnt skin. She sat near my desk where I could keep a close eye on her.

Art supplies were dispensed, and everyone was quiet for a few minutes. Ethan started mooching a quite soon into the activity though. Clearly displaying signs of ADHD, I was not allowed to advise his parents to get this assessed, despite it meaning that he would get extra support in the classroom (and playground). Besides, with the fact we were in the middle of a pandemic, GPs had more to worry about than a referral to child and adolescence services. So instead, I had to encourage him to settle down.

Today he had chosen that this wasn't an option, seeing as he'd had several weeks of being allowed to run around his house whenever he felt the urge. His parents were great, and apologetic whenever he got into trouble, but obviously didn't sign up to have to provide 24/7 care of a hyperactive child during times when you couldn't even take him to the park to let off steam. Re-introducing traditional schooling to him was going to be very challenging.

"Ethan, please sit down," was the most I was allowed to do.

No bribery, blackmail, touching or even going too near him was allowed. He chose to ignore me, of course. I managed to direct his attention to the small box of toy cars at the other end of the classroom and headed back to the other 30 children.

Ella already had glue on her hands, so I sent her to the sink to wash them. She stood by the basin twirling in circles.

"Miss," a little voice piped up.

I looked down. It was a glittery Grace.

"Oh, Grace."

I escorted her over to the basin, narrowly avoiding Ella's glued-up hands, partly peeled. Ella made a beeline for me, hugging me in my new summer dress that I had bravely chosen to wear to celebrate going back to work. Now covered in glitter AND glue, all 3 of us washed our hands whilst singing that bloody annoying song that had been on tv for what seemed like a lifetime.

Grace had glitter everywhere; her hair, her ears, mouth. I managed to persuade her to open her mouth and all seemed clear in there, for now! Paper towels wiped off a little more, and we all ventured back to the rest of the group.

I took matters into my own hands and collected all of the remaining glitter that I could find, hiding it in the back of the art cupboard, on the top shelf where Grace couldn't reach it. I encouraged all of the children to put their masterpieces somewhere safe to dry and then asked them to clean their tables. More paper towels seemed to do the trick for most of the mess. I chose to ignore the floors - 'not my job' I laughed to myself.

Playtime gave me just enough time to grab a coffee and clean the tables a little better than they had managed to.

Maths was next on the agenda, according to the lesson planning I had spent the majority of my time off organising. Today I hoped to teach them to count to 40, with the hope of eliminating any stupid rhymes for washing their hands, otherwise it was going to be a very long and slow term! Avoiding gender inequality, I encouraged girls as well as boys to embrace the 'maths monitors' role - I sure needed to think of something more fun to call them than 'monitors' - and allocated Lara, Joshua and Miles to hand out the counting games, one for each table.

Of course, 'winning wasn't as important as taking part' meant that we'd have to celebrate every move of each game.

Frustration wasn't just the name of a game during maths lesson, that's for sure. Luckily, the popper that shook the dice kept that table happy, as long as they took it in turns.

For Snakes and Ladders we had to call out "weeeeee, yaaaay," every time someone slipped down a snake, as it was no longer to be a negative thing to happen.

Snap was a new addition to the class. It had previously been a game similar to Tiddlywinks, until I found that Oscar had been putting the counters in his mouth last term. We seriously could have counted to 40 quite quickly back then, as he deposited them, along with more than enough drool, into my hands! Instead, simple playing cards with pictures and dots on was used.

All games rules included no touching, of course, which would be interesting for Snap, as they tended to end up slapping hands to win. I had pulled tables together, so that there were 10 children per table (Ethan was too busy hiding under my desk to participate, although he would have loved these games if he tried).

We set up all the chairs so they were a small distance away from the tables, and only the player could stand up and play their go. The children, of course, decided that they preferred to stand up to see, so I encouraged them to stand behind their chairs. For each turn, the child had to count out the results, by counting steps along the board or dots on the cards.

This was actually working quite well, for once. No-one was getting aggressive, and even Ethan took a look and counted along at times. Splitting the girls up, in particular Cerise, Grace and Ella, wasn't quite as ingenius as I thought it would be, as all games activities were now covered in glitter from their grubby hands!

Each table only had one round of the game they had been allocated, and once it was finished they had to join the spectators of the other games until all had completed. I asked them all to help pack away, but leave the games on my desk so that I could clean them. Their half-arsed efforts left counters, cards and dice strewn mostly over my desk, as the bell for lunch went and they dashed on their way to the playground. I couldn't care less what the plan was for the dinner hall, at least they were out of my hair for an hour!

The staffroom was only open for passing teachers wishing to make drinks or store their food in the fridge. I chose to avoid it altogether and got my lunchbox and an energy drink out of my bag, and pushed the games shit along to the corner of my desk for a little extra space. I grabbed my phone too and scrolled through social media whilst I ate. I regretted making finger food this morning for my lunch, as soon every mouthful seemed to have pink glitter on it – good job Cerise wasn't here! I had some wipes in my desk drawer, so I set about wiping down everything I could see that had glitter on it, then put it all away, just in time for round 3 of the classroom lessons.

It is a well-known fact that children learn more in the mornings than afternoons, so my lesson-planning usually consisted of art (but we'd already done that – should have waited until now to do that!), PE and music. I decided on music, to get some decent songs in their heads for handwashing.

My 'music monitors', yes, I really needed something better than 'monitor', were Sydney, Lucas and Ethan. Yes, it was a risky move with Ethan, but he loved banging on the drums. Recently sanitised percussion instruments were handed out to each child. This was going to be noisy. I had managed to convince the children that they didn't need to sit on the carpet (as they would be too close to each other) or at their tables (otherwise they'd just bang the instruments on the tables), so I instructed 10 children to sit on the carpet, with another 10 dragging their chairs over to sit behind the first 10, and then the last 10 were to stand behind the seated musicians. Ethan was quite happy with the drum set near the coat rack, which acted as a little soundproof area. His participation to the lesson would depend upon his cooperation, coordination and compliance.

Each group of ten children were encouraged to bang, tap, shake or similar their chosen instrument 4 times, one after the other. Four is an easy number for them, so there weren't too many errors here. After everyone had completed, I repeated the activity, but this time the children had to count along with the 'musician'. For the third round, I got them to count through each row, equalling FORTY. GENIUS!

At the end of the lesson, they all put their instruments back in the box, as Sydney and Lucas walked round with it, holding it at arm's length. They were all now ready to be sanitised before the next lesson. Ethan stayed with the drums until it was time for the children to collect their bags and wait for the home time bell. They had to leave the building in stages, so they lined up in 3 lines ready for their family members. I could see the relief on Ethan's mum's face when I didn't have to escort him out. She knew that this meant he had been well behaved today.

'Thank fuck today is over', I thought to myself, as the last of the children were collected. Only 5 weeks and 4 days left til the summer holidays!

I tidied up the classroom a bit, pushed in all the chairs and washed more glitter off my hands.

***

Back at home, I collapsed on the sofa.

"Wine!" I demanded.

My girlfriend, Sandy dutifully obliged, bringing the glass and the bottle in with her from the kitchen.

"How has it been, then?" she asked, secretly knowing the answer.

I just grunted.

She leaned over to give me a kiss and laughed. "You have glitter in your hair and on your nose!"

"You're welcome," I replied, rubbing my head on hers. "Could be worse, could be nits!"

Nineteen

Thing had always been a bit tight financially for Louise and her daughter Jordan. Becoming a single mum at just nineteen would have been a struggle for anyone, but for Louise she had been stranded in a luxurious fully furnished rented apartment in the centre of town, and without any maintenance from her ex, or the government, she had been left with a dilemma; find a job and continue this lifestyle or move into something more affordable. Unfortunately, matters were taken out of her hands when the apartment was unceremoniously evicted.

Their life had been idyllic up to that point, with Mark bringing home a more than decent wage and Louise not needing to work. However, Mark's sudden arrest for dealing drugs and money laundering soon burst their bubble.

It had been tough for Jordan too, as Mark had taken her to the park to play when the police busted him. He had tried to tell them that his nineteen-month-old daughter was on the baby swings, but they weren't interested, and as a result Jordan had been left alone for several hours, until one of the other mums in the park had noticed her crying, with no parent present; how was such a young baby meant to tell police officers what had happened, where she lived or who she was? A frantic Louise had eventually been reunited with her daughter after screeching down the phone at several authorities.

Louise decided from this point on that she would never leave her daughter with another person – EVER! As a result of these antics, although Jordan should have been too young to remember, she was cursed with separation anxiety, so extreme that not even other family members could console her if Louise left the room without her.

Looking back, it was probably more Louise's anxiety rubbing off on her infant daughter, but as Jordan grew up she rarely left her side. School had been unsuccessful, so Louise had chosen to home-school her instead. This meant that Louise was, although grateful for every penny she received, left to survive on the pittance that the government paid her. The more isolated the family became, the more intense the mental health issues became for Jordan. Playgroups were overwhelming for her, parks were avoided at all cost – in fact, when outdoors Louise had to avoid Jordan even looking at any type of play area, otherwise she would become hysterical with fear. Indeed, Louise had made a rod for her own back!

Louise eventually resorted to speaking to professionals; the world of social media and the 'experts' on anything.

"Send her to school! She'll cry for a bit, but she'll be better for it in the long run."

"She's controlling your life, bite the bullet now and get her socialising."

"Get her assessed for autism."

That last bit of advice attracted Louise's attention, preferring them over the distress of going to school (was it her distress she was avoiding or her child's though?). Several trips to the health centre were uneventful. No medication would be suitable, especially for a child so young. Eventually, Jordan was referred to a child therapist.

"She just needs to learn to deal with life!" was the outcome.

Louise was left to her own devices again and chose to continue with the home-schooling, or rather allowing her daughter to follow any hobbies that she was interested in, along with the use of the local library's computers for internet work.

Once Mark was released from prison, he attempted to make contact with his estranged girlfriend and daughter. Louise refused at first; how could she trust a man who had chosen an illegal career which caused all of this grief in the first place? Mark, however, had been 'blessed' with many professionals since leaving prison, including a social worker. Said social worker decided to intervene, believing that a couple of supervised sessions a week would be beneficial to all parties; Mark would be able to reconnect that father:daughter bond, and Louise could get a part-time job, along with the maintenance that Mark would now pay her. Unsure of whether Jordan would settle in the visitations, she put the search of a part-time job on a back burner.

During the first session, Jordan screamed constantly and was utterly distressed by the time she returned with the visitation supervisor. This continued for several weeks, with the girl becoming quite violent when separated from her mother, and this extended further until the child was constantly distressed. This time, the supervisor decided to arrange another therapy session for Jordan, to get to the root of the problem.

After 12 sessions of therapy, with Louise being present

but not participating, Jordan had been unable to get any closer to a 'cure'. The specialist had diagnosed her with PTSD and agoraphobia. Not quite correct, as Jordan loved being outdoors, with her mother of course. Unsatisfied with being unable to spend more time with his daughter, Mark soon dropped out of the scene, along with the maintenance payments. However, things finally started to look brighter as Jordan was awarded with a children's disability benefit (after many refusals in the past!), guaranteed for several years. This was a major breakthrough for the small family, as they no longer had to live on chicken nuggets or fishfingers as a cheap dinner. The specialist suggested more trips out, mingling with people but still being with her mum, so Louise splashed out on a new car, using part of the benefit to pay for it.

They toured beaches, zoos and botanical gardens, museums and castles, art galleries, restaurants and even Comicons. Jordan's interests in nature, history and art piqued and she soon began to flourish and gain confidence, so much so that at the age of fifteen she announced that she wanted to go to college to develop her artistic skills further than the internet and books could do. After several days of panic attacks, Louise agreed to take her to a college and see what their options were. The staff were very helpful and understanding and offered counselling services to assist the transition from home-education to the more formal college environment. After much discussion, it was agreed that college was possible, with the proviso that Louise drove her to there each day.

Jordan's sixteenth birthday came, as did a letter from the benefits department run by the government. The official document announced that now Jordan was sixteen, her disability payments would end, but that she could apply for the adult equivalent instead. A furious Louise rang them immediately, explaining that she had taken out a loan on the car, assured that the benefits would last until the loan repayments ended. They couldn't (or wouldn't?) help, except for offering to send out the application form for the new benefit, which would backdated if successful.

Louise completed the application form on behalf of Jordan, which was initially rejected by the benefits agency as they wanted to Jordan to complete the form herself, which she then dutifully did. A further letter arrived three weeks before college started, inviting her for an assessment interview. The nearest date available for the assessment was the day before college started.

Both ladies attended the interview, Jordan babbling incessantly about their new trips to fabulous locations, starting college and being happy in general. They would receive the decision 'in due course'. To celebrate college starting the next day, they both trawled around town after the interview to buy all the supplies that Jordan needed, along with some new autumn and winter clothes so that she could be as fashionable as her future peers. To top the day off, the girls decided to end their day with a trip to a local restaurant they had been wanting to visit for a few weeks now. Once they were full to the brim with delicious fine dining, an early night was required to ensure that Jordan was refreshed and well rested.

An anxious Louise didn't sleep at all well that night, and when she did finally submit, she woke early to find her daughter in bed with her; a regular habit for Jordan.

Louise managed to eventually drift off to sleep just in time for her alarm to beep. Several mugs of coffee were needed to be able to drive the new student to college, as a nervous Jordan approached the kitchen in her nervous state. Breakfast was refused, she was far too apprehensive and worried that the food would simply make a second appearance!

After several stops en route, with Jordan insisting that she felt sick, they finally arrived. A teaching assistant, Matilda, who had been allocated to accompany Jordan for as long as she was needed, was waiting at the entrance. Jordan reluctantly exited the car and they both slowly walked up to greet Matilda, who smiled to greet them.

Panic immediately settled in for Jordan, as she grabbed Louise's arm, not wanting her to leave.

"Mum, I can't do it!"

Louise was about to answer when Matilda interrupted, "Of course you can, Jordan. It's just a walk in the park!"

This set Jordan's anxiety off, with just the mere word 'park' causing her to have a full-blown panic attack on the college steps.

"Ok, this is going to take a little longer for the transitional phase," the special needs coordinator announced, once Jordan had recovered and been escorted, with her mother, to the office. "If you don't have any prior commitments, Ms Green, it may be best for you to accompany Jordan for the first few lessons, but sit out of the way so that she can benefit from the whole college experience."

He looked at Louise, who was worried for her daughter. Both then looked at Jordan.

"Yyyes, that should be ok, I haven't made any plans," Louise agreed.

Jordan nodded, and so both Matilda and Louise followed Jordan around for the remainder of the day.

This continued for two further days, until Matilda had earned the trust of both ladies.

As the weekend arrived, Louise had arranged a special trip to celebrate Jordan's first successful week at college; a visit to a new art exhibition at a top London gallery. Jordan was delighted. She took her notebook and sketch books, along with a digital camera borrowed from college so that she could record the events of the day. They stayed in a nearby hotel for the night and returned home on the Sunday afternoon.

As they arrived at home, there were several letters that had been delivered by the postie after they had left. Louise spotted the brown envelope with the disabilities benefit logo stamped on it. She opened it eagerly, but her excitement didn't last long when she discovered that they had refused the application; Jordan was no longer eligible, no longer disabled it seemed. Apparently, all of her excited babbling and being outdoors displayed that she no longer had agoraphobia OR PTSD! Louise was allowed to request a re-assessment within a month from the date of the letter. She would get onto that as soon as possible, but for now she didn't want it to affect the end of their fantastic weekend, so she put the letter away and they both headed to bed.

Jordan continued to flourish at college, passionately recounting the days' events to her mother. Behind the scenes though, whilst putting on a brave smile for her daughter, she secretly battled with the benefits office, who had denied her pleas for leniency. Eventually, just as Jordan was breaking up from college for the Christmas holidays, the money stopped. Luckily, Louise had bought the turkey and all the other trimmings needed for the holiday celebrations, so it wasn't something to worry about for now.

Of course, just because it wasn't something to worry about as nothing could be done over the Christmas period, Louise's anxiety wouldn't diminish so easily, and she spend every night writing out how much money they would have coming in, versus how much they would normally have. The figures weren't good, and no amount of juggling could sort it out.

For the next couple of months, Louise 'robbed Peter to pay Paul', an expression her mum had always used when they were in the exact same predicament. Just one slip up could knock down that house of cards. Using this method allowed her to keep the car for an extra month or two; she felt this was a priority over fishfingers or chicken nuggets for dinner, as Jordan would be unable to cope if her mother couldn't drive her to college.

However, the day soon arrived when Louise had to give back the car, despite paying for it for over three years – apparently during that period it is only the interest that would be paid, and only after that do the payments cover the cost of the car! Sure, it saved her the couple of hundred pounds a month, but how would it impact Jordan's health and education?

For the first few weeks Louise decided to accompany Jordan on the bus to college; Jordan had a free travel card, so it was only her own bus fare that she had to rummage the spare change jar to pay for. Easter came and went, and soon it was time for Jordan to venture out on her own.

Louise walked her to the bus stop on her first few days back at college, but soon the issues started to creep back. Jordan became very angry and violent most days, usually before leaving for college. Outbursts of screaming and crying, along with the occasional vomit caused issues. She vomited on the way to the bus stop, at the bus stop, on the bus, and this was assuming that she would get to college and stay there. She usually retuned home quite quickly, leaving Louise to have to ring college to report her absence. She missed lots of work, which made her even more anxious.

In the end, Louise ended up escorting her daughter to school on the bus for three years! Once Jordan had settled, she managed to acquire a small bubble of friends, who supported, understood and accepted her. A Job was still out of the question for Louise; who would hire someone with no job skills or experience, who had to do two school runs a day for her teenage daughter?! Luckily, she still had the small income allowance from the government. It wasn't much, but it kept a roof over their heads and food (albeit not particularly healthy) on the table.

Then Covid-19 hit, hard!

The impact didn't affect the family as much as it may have done for those who had well-paid full-time jobs, the government benefits stayed the same, so if anything, they saved money by not having to pay for Louise's 2 return bus tickets a day! However, Jordan's mental health dipped to an all-time low. She cried daily, worried for their lives if they should catch the virus; would they die? Would they become zombies? Would everyone else become zombies and attack them? Would there be riots and looting? Would it be the end of the whole human race?

Louise was drained from the reactions of her overwrought daughter, the constant reassurance, until one day, the announcement was made that lockdown was over, and students could return to their educational establishments. Jordan was so happy when she heard the news, insisting that she take the bus on her own. Louise was staggered, couldn't quite process it at first, but agreed that they should give it a try.

Once the college confirmed that it was re-opening, Jordan was fully ready to take this journey. She had received a text with a start date, and she was up and ready to leave before Louise had even emerged from her bed! Her friends had arranged to meet her at home and catch the bus together. When they arrived, she kissed her mum on the cheek and headed to the bus stop.

All day long, Louise was anxiously looking at her phone to make sure that there were no emergencies. She encouraged Jordan to message her when she arrived at school and when she left. Louise resisted the temptation to meet her at the bus stop, and this time she couldn't even treat her daughter to a celebratory slap-up meal, due to both Covid and lack of funds.

Jordan returned a lot earlier than expected on the following day, very tearful.

"College is done now," she announced.

"What do you mean, 'college is done'?" Louise replied, confused, as Jordan had only just gone back.

"They only needed us to go in to submit our work. That's it now."

The next day, she returned to her old habits of sitting in her bedroom; painting, drawing and listening to music. They continued to eat fishfingers and nuggets.

The summer of 2020 was milder than other years, but they had no funds or car to explore more of Britain's beautiful beaches and towns anyway.

Then, one day shortly before Jordan's nineteenth birthday another brown envelope appeared through the letter box. Louise opened it apprehensively. It was from the government benefits department, informing her that all of their benefits would expire at the end of August, unless Jordan continued her education!! Dumbfounded, she sat on her own and just re-read the letter. In less than one month there would be no more money.

She rang the college for advice, in case Jordan did want to complete her education but there was no answer. She looked on the college website. Free education for 16-18-year-olds. So that meant that Louise would have to pay for Jordan to return to college. She rang the benefits office, no reply there either, so she checked their website too. 'The benefits can be extended for up to six months, if the young adult registers with a careers advice centre'.

Great, a light at the end of the tunnel, Louise thought. She clicked the link provided, only to discover that they were closed too.

It seemed like nineteen-year-olds had managed to slip through the government's net; 'furloughs', 'eat out to help out' and job guarantees were all well and good if you weren't a nineteen-year-old with special needs who was unable to go back to college, not eligible to claim any job-seeking benefits or indeed get a job with her art qualifications, during Covid. The same applied to Louise, who had been the main caregiver all of her adult life, and had no work experience or qualifications either!

Cheer for the New Year

"Next year is going to be so much better than this year has been," Donna stated, to no-one in particular.

She had organised a small party, as she did every year. The texts had been sent, food had been bought, and alcohol... ok, so alcohol had been a bit more difficult to organise as she kept drinking it; it had been a stressful year. BYOB had been added to all the texts, so that solved that problem!

Her little council flat was heaving with inebriated twenty-somethings last year, and she expected the same again tonight. She gave the whole place a massive clean and then set about preparing the little 'horse derves', as she put it. Mini pizzas & burgers, sausage rolls, mince pies, a couple of cheesecakes and 'gattows', and 'chocolatey claires'; NO SALAD, diet starts tomorrow.

She had invited about 40 to the party, but some were just as a gesture as she knew they wouldn't come. She'd tried to invite a few 'oldies' as she put it, like Jess who used to live in the flat downstairs, just to ensure that it wasn't just the same rowdy bunch from school. Work had been almost non-existent since 'The 'Rona', and a few of her regular mates had not kept in touch with her. She'd still invited them, just to show willing, even if she didn't know what their problem was.

She dragged a kitchen chair into the hallway and stood on it in her new fluffy leopard-print slippers to put up some banners and balloons with drawing pins. She'd chosen pink decorations this year, to match her Christmas tree.

Her mobile phone played an odd tune that she hadn't ever pre-set as an alarm, to tell her to get the food out of the oven and go and get ready. The sausage rolls needed longer, and they still looked way too pale, but that could have been because she couldn't be bothered to egg wash them first; she didn't know how to wash pastry in eggs! She slid all of the other cooked snacks onto serving plates and shoved the sausage rolls back in.

To keep with the theme, she had bought a pink sequinned dress. After a revitalising shower, she applied makeup, styled hair and slipped on the dress. 'Slipped on' is not really the correct phrase actually, as she had really piled on the pounds this year. Again, that wasn't the right phrase, as it had been about 2 stone, one of which appeared after the first month off work. Without the daily walk to work and back, and the weekly dancing sesh out clubbing with her mates, she hadn't managed to do all of her steps every day. Mind you, her smart watch disagreed with that ever since she discovered that the 'steps' mounted up simply by moving her arm, so she just ate and drank even more! Luckily, the dress was stretchy, albeit rather snug.

All ready to party, she connected the Bluetooth on her phone, connecting it to her sound bar and started with the tunes. She'd watched a lot of tv this year and hadn't really kept up to date with the latest chart music, so selected the 'Christmas Playlist' from her music provider app. She had a little jig around the open plan living space, pinching the odd sweet treat off a plate. She was pouring out some Prosecco into glasses when the door knocked.

'This is it!' she thought to herself, as she popped a strawberry cream chocolate into her mouth. It was Ellie, her bestie. They had been joined at the hip since school and Donna knew 'her girl' wouldn't let her down. They embraced and headed back to the fizz and comestibles.

"Oooh, 'secco, lavely!" Ellie announced with delight.

She pulled a punnet of strawberries out of the carrier bag she was holding. "These'll go well nice wiv it."

She popped a couple in each of the glasses and their fizz was reinvigorated. Donna downed it in one, strawberry and all!

"Lash, Els," she responded as she topped up the glasses again, adding more of the fruit.

The door knocked again, and Donna squealed.

"Ding Dong, Avon calling," she giggled as she dashed over to the door.

"Awright, Dons," a variety of voices piped up.

Donna invited them in.

"I bought some 'secco," Deena announced as she took her coat off.

"Just sling it on the bed, hun," Donna replied. "The coat, not the 'secco!"

They all cackled with laughter, as Ellie topped up more glasses and added the special ingredient. This went down like a ton of bricks. Donna opened some savoury snack bags and poured the contents into her giant gold pasta bowls.

More guess arrived, including Donna's boyfriend, Albie, and his mum.

"You told me you needed more oldies this year, so I brought Mum," he explained. "She's been ever so lonely since Dad passed away the other month."

He crossed his chest and kissed the cross which was hanging off a huge gold belcher chain around his neck.

"Well, I've invited a few more oldies, so hopefully we can fix 'er up wiv someone," Donna replied.

Albie's mum, Fiona, was a quiet lady at the best of times, and her nerves were shot to pieces since her husband perished 'as a result of the Corona virus', as the official report stated. Donna ushered her through and instructed everyone to clear the sofa so that she could sit down.

"Everyone, this is Fonia," she announced, "Albie's mum."

"It's Fiona," Fiona corrected.

Donna nodded. "You want 'secco?"

Fiona looked puzzled. Donna grabbed a glass and passed it to her, but she shook her head. "I'd prefer tea, if you have any?" Fiona suggested.

Donna nodded again, and loudly entered the kitchen, asking people to move out of the way so she could get to the kettle. "Albie's mum wants tea. What a lav, bless 'er."

A fresh batch of young blood arrived while Donna was busy in the kitchen making Fiona's tea. Ellie let them in.

"ELS!" one of them cried. "Not seen ya for yonks, babe,

how ya doin'?"

"Hiya, what's up?" she replied.

She led them all into the small living area. Donna greeted them with Fiona's tea.

"You got no plonk, Don?" Tanya enquired, laughing sarcastically.

"Naaa, Tarn, it's for Albie's mum, bless 'er. She ain't got no-one to spend New Year wiv, so Albie brought her along."

"Awww bless 'er 'art. I could ask me gramps if he wants to come; He ain't got no-one eever?"

"Awww bless 'im. Yeh ask 'im. Don't want too many oldies 'ere though. We're meant to be 'ere to celebrate."

The night continued with much fun and laughter. Bottles of Prosecco were drained in minutes and soon they had to resort to a keg of lager which someone that Donna didn't know had brought.

Fiona nursed the same cup of tea that had been given to her when she arrived, too shy to ask for more. The grandad who was invited by one of Donna's friends declined the offer, but another friend of theirs, Jake, sat next to Fiona and kept her company.

"I don't know anyone here, I came here wiv Gem, but she's facked off with some bloke," the young chap explained.

'Gem' was Gemma, Donna's friend from work, who Donna discovered frolicking with this 'bloke' on her bed, and promptly evicted them both. Jake managed to avoid eviction. He continued to sit on the sofa next to his new mate, and pulled a small pot of, well... pot out of his pocket and casually rolled a huge joint. Knowing better than to spark up in the room, he compromised by opening the front window and leaning out.

Fiona stared at him, Jake wasn't sure what kind of stare it was, so offered her a toke. She scrunched her nose up and shook her head. They maintained eye contact for a few more minutes and he re-offered the smoke.

"My husband died a few months ago of 'respiratory failure related to COVID'," she explained.

"So sad to hear that, babe. Tobacco does the damage, this doesn't," he replied.

She stood up and took a small drag. She had smoked a lot when she was younger, tobacco and weed, and this felt good. Feeling a little more relaxed, she grabbed a bowl of onion rings and a half bottle of white wine, as all of the Prosecco was gone. Both of them returned to the sofa and swigged wine straight out of the bottle. Jake placed an onion ring between his lips, expecting Fiona to take it out with her mouth.

"I'm newly widowed," she reminded him.

"I'm sure he wouldn't mind," he replied, "besides, I fancy your son, not you," he admitted bravely.

"He'd punch your lights out," she giggled.

"Which one?" he asked.

"Both of them!"

As if on cue, a fight broke out between Gemma, who had managed to creep back in, and the girlfriend of whom Gemma had been caught in the bedroom. It started in the hall as Gemma re-entered, but spilled out into the living room, and concluded around the sofa. The other girl, whose name nobody seemed to know, fell against Fiona and knocked her wine bottle over. Fiona erupted. On her feet in seconds, she had a hold of this girl's hair, and threw a punch right at her.

"That was MY wine, BITCH!" she exclaimed, as the girl got back onto her feet.

The fight was broken by Jake and Albie, who escorted both Gemma and her young adversary outside, just in time for the police to arrive. They had been called by neighbours who were complaining about the noise, the smell of weed and now the fight. It was different now that Donna's old neighbours had moved out, and this new lot were less tolerant to almost anything. Both girls were taken into custody and Jake and Albie returned to the party.

"I suppose that's one good thing wiv the grumps downstairs," Donna laughed.

All drama over, they all stood together in the living area as they watched the tv channel which was broadcasting live from London, awaiting Big Ben to announce the new year.

"Ten, nine, eight..." they all participated in the countdown and cheered when Big Ben chimed.

There was a pause, like everyone was expecting something spectacular as 2020 was behind them.

"I can smell burning," Fiona announced.

"MY SAUSAGE ROLLS!" Donna screamed, dashing to turn the oven off.

Every Cloud

"...So in summary, Silver Lining Holidays should be up and running by the end of Lockdown Two."

The video conference call went silent. Elise Silver panicked ever so slightly; were they mulling it over or had the videos frozen, she wondered.

This was an important call for Elise. The last four months of the world's second lockdown had been busy thinking time for the young entrepreneur. During the first lockdown, she had pined to get away to somewhere warm and sunny, except during those couple of days of warm weather in England, when she wished she was back in Iceland. She was a frequent flyer, well to be precise, a frequent traveller. She'd never been keen on the flying and had done her level best to visit as many parts of the world by alternative means. Obviously this put a limit on many places, but now she saw it as an opportunity to explore other parts of the world doing just that, avoiding flying!

Dozens of notebooks were piled in corners of her 'bedroom', as she had planned and re-planned her new business venture. Re-writing over and over again until everything was perfect. All she needed now was funds, which was the reason behind this call that morning. Usually when Elise had one of her mad, or rather, enterprising plans, she kept it to herself. She was rarely taken seriously, and even if she was, she knew that there was a chance that someone would steal her idea and profit from all of her hard work. Thank goodness for the internet, without which Elise would have not been able to do even a fraction of the research that she had completed, to the point of even having a patent pending. No-one was going to ridicule her with this venture, it was watertight.

Elise had started this latest project sooner than she realised, by simply following her mantra of avoiding planes. She had converted an old ambulance into a camper van, ripping out everything and starting with a blank canvas. Using recycled products for everything she built into the recreational vehicle, it was the perfect size for Elise to drive, and sleep comfortably; she even kept the light on the roof (although she had to remove the siren and electrical wires that connected it, for legal reasons)! Her first few trips had been quite close to home, to give her time to combat any fears that she may have had. But before long she had vacated her little flat and was living in the motor home and travelling to everywhere that connected the UK by road (or the English Channel).

First, Wales, to that well-known place with the very long name: Llanfairpwll-gwyngyllgogerychwyrndrob-wllllantysiliogogogoch.

Next, Scotland, to the North Coast 500, where she saw the aurora borealis in all of its glory.

Gibraltar connected Europe to Africa, and her expeditions continued, sticking to roads and tour guide books to avoid scary predators!

Collecting stickers from each new place to embellish the exterior of her van, she also had a small map of the world framed on one of the ambulance's small interior walls, with a pin stuck in every place she had visited. Photos of 'Amber' the ambulance were taken by every landmark that they could get close to, and Elise blogged whenever possible. She savoured the local cuisine and wished that she could 'bottle' the smells; the food, flora, the smell from the heat, which was something that she just couldn't explain.

She had saved as much money as possible, both before she started travelling, and by being frugal when she was out on the open road. After a while, her blog 'A&E: Amber and Elise' achieved the attention she hoped, and she earned a little to expand her voyages. Any extra money she needed was earned by selling her handmade aromatherapy packs in local markets.

She loved nothing more than to wake up, switch on the kettle and open her blinds to see the most magnificent views from the ambulance's back windows. And the windows were still blacked out, so no-one could see her morning hair!

The pandemic, however, had brought her travelling to a head. Luckily, she had been parked on her parents' driveway in the UK when lockdown struck, and there she stayed until the summer. As there was so much unrest with the global virus, she continued her travels but within the UK again, and had to re-return to 'Driveway le Chez Silver' when northern counties started to enter tier three. It was then that the planning began.

With nowhere to go and an abundance of essential oils, she started dabbling and tweaking until she had managed to recreate the smells that had tantalised her senses. The internet provided her with recipes of many dishes from around the globe, and online shopping gave her the opportunity to buy the ingredients. An MP3 player allowed her to store sounds from around the globe, along with the ambience of local markets, restaurants and wildlife. A virtual reality headset would provide the visual atmosphere. All that was left was a trial run to see if all of her planning would survive the 'parent test'.

Elise's parents had always encouraged her to follow her dreams, but were a little apprehensive when she offered them the 'opportunity' of a 'Virtual Vacation of a Lifetime'. A spare room was all that she needed to complete the 'experience' of 'A Weekend in Morocco', oh, and the spare reclaimed wood she had stored in their garage, along with an old sandpit. And some Moroccan rugs.... Wow this was going to need a little more preparation after all!

First things first, using recycled plastic bags she lined the whole of the floor in the room that her parents had emptied of old furniture and suitcases purely for this great adventure. Ensuring it was watertight (and sandtight) she separated the floor into three sections; one for sand, one for water and one for a bed. Two deckchairs that had previously hung on the back of Amber were set up on the sand. The MP3 player was plugged in, along with Elise's aromatherapy diffuser.

Mr and Mrs Silver apprehensively entered their 'luxury apartment' and the experience began. Conditions were cramped, and it was a struggle for their only child to answer their every whim and desire; after all, this was a two-night, all-inclusive break for them. Market traders shouted in the distance, offering their wares. The Silvers wanted to buy one of the rugs (which they actually owned already!) and Elise clicked the 'barter: Morocco' file on the MP3 and a deal was sealed. Dinner was couscous and Zaaluk was served on the terrace (Elise had cleverly managed to clear away the sand for the evening, and replace with more wood as flooring whilst her parents were at 'the market').

At the end of the weekend, the young entrepreneur apprehensively waited for their feedback. She had never really been good at receiving criticism, which had been an awful shame growing up with the worst critics ever, Barb and Glen Silver; she braced herself.

"Well, dear, that certainly was an experience," Barb began.

"Yes, the souk was rather interesting, the trade didn't quite go as we expected," Glen agreed.

"Yes," Elise replied, "it does need some tweaks. On a scale of one to ten, how authentic did it feel?"

"Elise, dear, it was a weekend in our spare room, but yes, I can see what you were aiming to achieve."

Elise waited patiently, for more feedback, or indeed the marks out of ten.

"Well then, time for a cup of tea, eh Glen?"

"Yes dear, that mint tea was nice, very much like what we had in the Bedouin tents in 2013 when we went on the stargazing trip in the Sinai Desert, but Elise's tent and cushions were far more comfortable!"

"Yes, and no camel ride, or armed guards, thank goodness!"

Was that a positive?

"I still need some paracetamol for my back though," Barb concluded, as they skipped the 'plane home' and wandered straight into the kitchen.

Obviously, Elise was not going to visit customers and wreck their spare rooms, should they even have one. The grant/loan was to purchase and renovate a double decker bus. Using the downstairs as the 'outdoors', and upstairs as the 'apartment', she knew she could make the experience perfect. If her parent enjoyed, well maybe enjoyed wasn't the word, but *understood* the thoughts behind it, then any customer would!

It was just left to the investors to decide now. The anxious silence was deafening.

The first of the three investors broke the silence.

"Thank you, Miss Silver. Unfortunately, I have concerns about the demographics. You mentioned that you could expand the business by developing franchises. For 'ambassadors' around the world to offer the same experiences as you, which in theory sounds great, and a great opportunity for you to earn more money, but they won't all be able to buy a double decker bus and renovate it. And even if they could, the franchisees may not renovate to the standard you would do yourself, which could damage your reputation. I'm afraid it's not something I can consider right now."

Elise felt downhearted but thanked him for his time. She knew it was the polite thing to do, although she just wanted to rant at him.

Next, was the only lady in the panel.

"Hello, Elise. Yes, I must agree with Dennis. It's just not feasible, sorry."

"Thank you, Sarah," Elise responded.

"Miss Silver, Elise, it sounds very exciting. Sure, right now it may not be the most luxurious of holidays, and the only market research you could do was with your parents. I, we, appreciate your honesty. I can see the potential in this project, as well as the points that my esteemed peers have pointed out.

"People in the UK sure could do with a holiday, whether they want warm and sunny or cold and picturesque. A small vacation is better than no holiday at all.

"I can't agree to pay the full amount, but if you can find an investor who can pay half, then I will match it."

Elise stuttered as she spoke, "Ok, thanks, Leo. Obviously, right now I haven't managed to find another investor. Is it possible to allow me to have some time to find someone, please?"

Leo smiled. "Yes, of course. I shall email you my details along with the offer I have made."

"Thank you all, for taking the time to listen and consider my proposal. I appreciate your feedback and honesty."

"You're welcome," Dennis replied, and then disappeared from the screen.

"Good luck, both," Sarah said, cancelling the call at her end.

"Look forward to working with you, Elise," Leo concluded.

A million things were running through Elise's mind on her journey home with Amber. Who could she get to match Leo's offer? The bank had refused, the lady from her networking group (who was a travel agent with no work) declined a partnership. The further she went on her journey home, the less confident she became. There was no-one.

As she returned home, she walked sullenly into the kitchen where her parents usually resided. They were gathered around the stove, concocting delicious cuisine in their old tagine. It smelled amazing. In all that running around, she had failed to eat *anything*, partly due to nerves too. Her tummy rumbled instantly.

"Oh, hello, dear," her mum greeted her.

"Hi Mum, Dad."

"Oh, that isn't a happy face," Dad observed.

"Well, you can't win them all," their daughter shrugged.

She explained the situation in fully, whilst holding a mug of coffee and slurping at it until it cooled.

"Well, that's not so bad," Barb stated. "I thought you were going to say they all said no!"

"Two and a half said no, Mum," she laughed bitterly, fighting back the tears.

Barb turned back to the stove and started dishing up the food.

Her parents continued to be jovial as they all ate, and Elise found herself smiling at their antics. They had been married for over 25 years, yet still appeared to be very happy with the arrangement.

"Our 'weekend in Morocco' brought back some lovely memories of our honeymoon," Barb explained.

"Aww that's lovely," Elise replied, beaming at them. "If that's the case, I feel like I have succeeded."

"Yes, your idea was a good one, it just needs more planning," her mother continued. "So we will contribute the other half of the money that you need, to help you to fine tune everything, as long as you let us help you. It didn't seem like a good idea at first, and sleeping in the corner of our spare room wasn't ideal, but we can see the idea behind it."

"Ohhhh!" Elise radiated, "are you sure?"

"It'll come out of your inheritance, dear," her dad smiled.

She stood up, knocking her chair over and hugged them both.

"Time for a new notebook!"

Masquerade Ball

"Have you got everything that you need, Joni?"

"Yes, Mum," Joni replied impatiently.

The masquerade ball to celebrate the end of 2021, in lieu of the school prom (due to frequent lockdowns) was a genius idea by the school council, of which Joni played a small part. To raise funds for the school, to improve the school's infirmary, the council members' artistic division made a selection of full-face masks, which all attendees of said ball HAD to wear.

Joni wore an elaborate carnival mask, and dressed in bright, vibrant colours to celebrate the diversity of her hometown and the large population of inhabitants from the Caribbean.

"The car is waiting outside, darling," her mum announced. "Do you have your phone ready?"

Joni nodded, as she retrieved the phone from her little bag, handmade to replicate a pineapple, and opened up the C19 app. She held her spare hand to her mouth and blew an invisible kiss, leaving with a dramatic swish of her dress. She walked to her front garden gate and waited patiently for the Medical Officer Connor to arrive, to clear her to leave.

There weren't many people booked in to leave their homes this evening, and the wait didn't take too long. Joni still felt the need to pull on her little shrug as a barrier to the bitter December air.

"Good evening, miss. Can I have your details please?"

She held up my phone and pointed the app at his reading device. It beeped and turned green.

"Thank you, Joni," he continued, reading the details on his reader. "Mask?"

All of their ID showed images with and without masks, but this only included the regular compulsory nose and mouth masks. He stepped back a couple of paces while she removed her mask and smiled.

"Excellent," he confirmed. "You are free to enter the car now."

He stepped to the side to allow Joni to approach the black cab. She re-scanned her phone on the panel at the side of the rear passenger door. It beeped and a green circle appeared on the panel and her phone simultaneously. She added a squirt of hand sanitiser from the dispenser attached to the door as the passenger door clicked, allowing the teenager to enter.

"Hi, Joni," a white plague doctor greeted her.

"Jesus!" Joni exclaimed.

"It's just me, Laurel," she giggled excitedly, lifting her mask so that her friend could identify her through the glass screen.

"Loz, of all the masks you could have chosen....."

"Too soon?" she laughed sarcastically.

"I thought you would have gone for something more feminine, at least."

"Just a couple more pickups, ladies," the driver announced.

"Thank you," the girls said synchronously, and giggled again.

Prom was an important rite of passage for all teenagers, but more so this year, as they were celebrating life as survivors of the pandemic. The girls chattered eagerly throughout the whole journey. Two young men were picked up en route, both dressed as court jesters, and sat opposite Joni and Laurel, behind their own screens.

There were several staff members at the entrance when the four youths arrived. The girls' cab door opened first, allowing them to approach the teachers with gusto.

"Steady on, ladies," the head, Mrs Bloom stated, "you still have to pass our security system yet."

She gestured for them to enter the first door, where the two friends reapplied the cool, gloopy gel to their hands and placed their bags in the sanitised container that travelled through the x-ray machine. They stepped through the full body scanners and retrieved their bags on the other side. The panel on the second door flashed green and the door unlocked.

A sea of glitter, feathers and sequins greeted them as an array of masked teens danced in the centre of the school hall. Lights flashed in time to the music. The DJ on stage was Mr Jones, who was the crush of the majority of the girls present tonight, and most of those were dancing as close to the stage to attract his attention. Very few knew that he was actually in a relationship with the English teacher, Mr Jeffries. He still liked the attention of the girls, though.

Joni and Laurel headed to the soft drink bar and requested a cola each. The school wasn't cool enough to serve branded drinks, but then again, it was a free bar, so they couldn't really complain. They sipped their warm, flat drinks out of reusable paper cups, and approached the main area. Ms Bainbridge beamed at them both.

"Remember, no physical contact. Although everyone has been tested negative, we aren't taking any chances."

This was a necessity, since the government had quashed school parties unless the stringent security procedures were adhered to. As the general public could only be tested for Covid once a week, due to financial restraints, it was still possible for attendees to be positive but without symptoms There were hopes for the future to install devices outside all residential premises to detect the virus before an individual could leave their home, but this was a long way off.

Fancy gloves sealed in reusable plastic bags were handed out to each person who arrived at the party. Joni had ordered yellow arm length satin gloves, and Laurel had black lacy gloves, (with a clear protective lining) that only reached her wrists. Both were deemed suitable for the event. Ms Bainbridge checked their masks to ensure they complied with the rules, and they were granted entrance.

***

Back at home, Joni's mother was trying her hardest to have a good New Year's Eve, but had lost the majority of her family and friends to Covid. She wandered sullenly over to her iPad, and after a few clicks, she was connected to the remainder of her online family.

"Is Joni in there with you, Kay?"

"No, Grandma, she's at a school party."

Grandma gasped. "But she can't, it's far too dangerous!"

"No, it's fine, Grandma," Kay insisted, "they have all the required safety procedures in place. The local authority gave them permission. They are being monitored by the Incident Reserve Police. She will be fine."

"We have to give the poor girl a life, Joan," Great-Aunt Doris chided her sister. "There's little left in life for the younger ones. We could play out in the street when we were younger. Poor Joni has already lost her father and two of her friends. It's no life for a teenager."

"At least she won't get in the family way for a while," Joan replied.

Kay decided to change the subject. "Have you all got your bubbly ready, ladies?"

"I couldn't open the bottle," Joan replied despondently.

"Oh, Gran," Kay sighed.

"I have sherry," Joan announced, "that will do fine."

"It sure will, Joan," Doris agreed.

"Joni should be back before midnight, so we can toast to 2022 then."

"Good, Good," Joan replied.

"Have you both got the film ready?" Doris enquired.

"Yes, I have," Kay replied. "Gran?"

"Yes, dearie," Joan replied.

"We'll synchronise in 60 seconds."

All three counted down from 60 and clicked their remotes, and the title music started in stereo, through the iPads and the soundbars they had. They dimmed their lights and settled down with pretzels, popcorn and chocolate.

***

The party was in full swing at Kennedy Secondary School. The teachers were patrolling all areas of the hall to ensure that none of the teenagers were close enough to touch.

"It's like Grease all over again," Matt Jones joked with Ian Jeffries, who had approached the DJ stage whilst inspecting girls who were slavering over his life partner. "No touching, people," he mimicked the headteacher character from the 1970s film.

They both laughed. Ian slipped his mask back down over his face and headed over to the toilets. Joni was standing in a queue waiting for the next available cubicle. Surprisingly, there wasn't a constant supervisor keeping an eye on them all, just the occasional teacher as part of their designated route. Joni smiled at this. A little trust never hurt anyone. She dragged her foot over the sticker on the floor that indicated where to queue until the next person entered the toilets. Laurel was behind her, whispering to her friend.

"I really need to go," she whined.

Joni shrugged her shoulders. "I suppose you can swap with me if you want?"

"Na man, it's cool. I'm going to nip into the mens', there's no-one waiting in there."

"Loz, you can't do that!"

"Watch me!" she smirked as she snuck off.

Two cubicles became vacant at the same time and Joni dashed in.

When she came out, Laurel still hadn't resurfaced from the grim toilets of the opposite gender. She could see Mr Jeffries disappearing back to the bar for a drink top up and took this opportunity to peer into the men's room and give a little shout out.

"Loz," she whispered, as she stood by the door.

There was no answer, so Joni took a tentative step further in.

"Loz," she whispered, louder than the first time.

Still no answer, so she stepped in completely and peeped under the doors of the cubicles. The first two were empty, but the one at the far end showed a little of Laurel's black and white chiffon dress.

"Loz!" Joni muttered through gritted teeth. "Unless you're ill, you need to get out of here before someone sees you."

"I'm ill then," was the flippant reply.

There was more than one voice that tittered behind the door. Joni put her full weight against the door and managed to open it, just in time to catch Laurel and a lad called Oliver from the other form in year 11 kissing.

"Loz," Joni yelled, "what the hell are you doing?! You know how dangerous this is!"

"YOLO," Oliver replied.

"YOLO," Joni screeched. "You could bloody die! Don't you know that a kiss is more deadly than unprotected sex?!"

"You could still die from unprotected sex," Oliver piped up. "Besides, we'll make sure we're protected."

"That's great," Joni spat bitterly. "So you won't catch HIV, but you could die from Covid in a matter of days!"

Not realising how loud she had become, Mr Jeffries stormed in.

"What the hell is going on in here!?" he yelled.

Joni was sobbing at this point, at the thought of her friend's behaviour as much as the fear of losing her, like most of her family. Oliver and Laurel were still in their embrace, Laurel with her mask pulled onto her head, and Oliver's generic superhero mask under his chin.

"I am so disappointed in you," Mr Jeffries continued, calling the on-call security team to assist in the 'special force's arrest', a slightly higher rank than the usual citizen's arrest.

In no time, the three adolescents were forced to take the walk of shame, escorted off the premises by the Reserves and frogmarched into the community hall for Covid testing and interrogation.

Joni decided not to say anything about what had happened, despite the way that her friend had treated her. Mr Jeffries, however, confirmed that she was merely a bystander attempting to bring some order to the situation. She was released without charge once the results confirmed that she was C-19 negative. She was bundled into a Reserves' car and taken home.

***

Back at home, Kay, Doris and Joan were ready to see in the new year. Kay didn't even realise that Joni was home until she heard the front door slam.

"That you, Joni?" her mother enquired.

She saw her daughter in floods of tears but wasn't allowed the opportunity to talk to her before she had locked herself in her room.

"No, Gran," Kay responded to her grandmother's questioning, "I didn't get the time to talk to her. I did get this note through the door though. It says that Joni was involved in a health breach but tested negative and was cleared of all charges."

"Will she be with us at midnight?"

"I don't know, I can ask...."

"It's midnight now," Doris announced.

Kay sighed, sad that she couldn't celebrate with her closest relation.

The ladies raised a glass.

"Here's to a new year, let's hope that it is better than the last one!" Doris toasted.

"They say that you should start the year as you mean to go on," Joan added.

And there they all remained, three generations of lonely and disappointed women, all in different rooms.

Auld Lang Syne

"Next year is going to be so much better than this year has been," Donna stated, to no-one in particular.

She had organised a small party, as she did every year. The texts had been sent, food had been bought, and alcohol... ok, so alcohol had been a bit more difficult to organise as she kept drinking it; it had been a stressful year. BYOB had been added to all the texts, so that solved that problem!

Her little council flat was heaving with inebriated twenty-somethings last year, and she expected the same again tonight. She gave the whole place a massive clean and then set about preparing the little 'horse derves', as she put it. Cocktail sausages, different flavoured crisps, sandwiches along with mince pies, a box of biscuits and she'd managed to nab the last of the chocolate mini rolls; NO SALAD, diet starts tomorrow.

She had invited about 20 to the party, but some were just as a gesture as she knew they wouldn't come. She would have invited poor Rachael, shame what happened to her. Albie was bringing his mum, Fiona, again, and her friend Jake, who she'd met at the party last year. She swerved away from his mate, Gemma, though, she was just trouble.

"Skank," Donna muttered to herself, as she thought about how Gemma had behaved last year.

She shook her head of the memory and focussed on getting ready for the party. She had bought some nice leggings to go under a short blue dress, which she laid on the bed while she had a shower.

All clean and dressed, with a little bit of foundation and mascara, Donna was ready for the festivities. All the food was out of the oven - nothing was going to get burned this year – and she switched on the tv to the channel that broadcasts the party celebrations.

They'd already celebrated the arrival of 2021 in Australia and the Far East, she learned, next they would bring satellite reports from Eastern Europe and then Western Europe would be after. She doubted she'd still be up for America's merrymaking as that would be hours later; although maybe she'd catch it when she got up, if she wasn't too hungover of course.

She opened a bottle of Bucks Fizz, just about all she had left over from Christmas, and poured herself a mug. She sat back on her sofa and tucked her feet, clad in thick woolly socks that her nan had knitted her, under the blanket, that her mum had made her. It was pink, chunky and fluffy, and apparently her mum had 'arm-knitted' it, but she didn't know what that meant. She fiddled about the gaping holes that were in it, which were intentional, not really paying attention to the tv. There was some tart on there shouting into the mic, clearly intoxicated, and this bored Donna.

A knocking at the door brought Donna back into the here and now. She smiled and wandered into the hall to greet the first of her guests. It was Albie, Jake and Fiona.

"'Ello, darlin's," she shrilled with fake excitement, fake kissing each visitor on each cheek, like the French do.

Albie passed her a bottle of Bucks Fizz. "I brought this from the shop," he explained. "Sorry, babe, this is all they had left in the supermarket, well apart from £125

Champagne, lol."

Donna smiled the best smile that she could. "That's ok, hun, it should be enough," she replied.

She was sure she could continue sipping out of her mugful, until someone brought some more booze.

"I brought some homemade 'special brownies'," Fiona announced, handing over a plastic tub. "Jake helped with some of the ingredients, if you know what I mean?!"

"Aww thanks Fonia, and Jake of course," Donna replied; Fiona didn't bother to correct her.

***

"So, tell me something, Donna," Fiona leaned over towards their hostess later that evening, "Why do you call me Fonia, rather than Fiona?"

"Oh, well, that's easy, ain't it? I 'ad a mate at school, her name was Sonia, and yours is spelt the same, so it's just natural queen's English. I was taught proper."

"But it's not spelled the same," Fiona replied.

"Donna laughed, "You're such a tease, Fonia!"

The door knocked again. Donna jumped up to answer it. It was her best friend since school, Ellie.

"Els," Donna squealed, air kissing both cheeks.

"You look pale, babe, you ok?" Ellie questioned.

"Yeah, just don't have my tans anymore, no point really," Donna replied.

"I got a bottle of Bucks Fizz from the offie, Don. It's all I could get…."

"apart from the £125 bottles of champers?" Donna finished her sentence for her.

"Yeah, how did you know?"

"Just a guess," Donna giggled.

No-one needed introductions, as they all met at last year's party. Ellie sat down with the others, and Donna handed round plates of food.

"No sausage rolls this year, Don?" Jake laughed.

"Naa, mate," she replied, and they all cackled with laughter.

"Get one of these down ya," Jake held out the brownie tub.

The second of the three bottles of Bucks Fizz was opened, and the guests grabbed a mug out of the cupboard, draining it in one serving.

"We're need to pace ourselves," Donna announced, "or we're not gonna have any alcohol left to toast the new year."

"Maybe the next lot of guests will have some?" Ellie suggested.

"Ok, fair dos, let's just go for it!"

They all sat in Donna's pink living room, crouching over the coffee table where the nibbles had migrated to. They filled their boots fairly quickly.

"Shit, we've eaten everyfink, what are the next ones gonna eat?" Donna exclaimed.

"Their fault for being late!" Albie replied.

"True," Donna replied, reaching for another brownie.

Coffee table cleared of empty plates by Fiona, she returned from the kitchen with a board game that she had found in one of Donna's cupboards.

"Yay!" they all cheered, as she set it up on the table.

"Shall we do the quick version, where you can buy any streets and stuff that you want on the first go round the board?" Fiona suggested.

"Can do," Donna replied, "that way we won't be acting rude when the rest turn up."

The game flowed briskly, with Donna losing first, followed by Albie in sympathy. In fact, despite the excessive amount of special brownies, Fiona won the game; the prize, the last mug of Bucks Fizz.

"There's only an hour til midnight, guys. I'm going to nip down to the other offie near where I live, and see if I can get some more booze," Albie offered.

"Don't worry about the offie, Alb, there's half a bottle of sherry in one of the cupboards in our kitchen," Fiona announced.

Albie was off, quicker than anyone could say 'Monopoly' correctly, returning in just fifteen minutes.

"Blimey, lav, you must have ran all the way!" Donna commended.

"Only for you, my beautiful lady!"

Albie topped all the mugs up to the brim, and they all downed it quickly.

At midnight, Big Ben's bells could be heard ringing on the tv. Fireworks were launched, although not as extravagant as last year, and people were cheering, both on tv and outside.

Donna, Ellie, Albie, Jake and Fiona were completely unawares though, as they were all fast asleep!

This World Has Been Hell Lately!

"Are there no biscuits?" I enquired, staring at the coffee pot, knowing that I'd have to stick with water.

"Der! We've been in lockdown for, like, forever!" a greasy-looking youth in a red baseball cap and a mask with a football team logo on explained.

"Shops are still open," I suggested.

"Biscuits went after the loo roll, flour and teabags."

"Don't forget the nappies," a second youth piped up.

"What do we need nappies for?"

Clearly I was in for a longer 'hour' than expected, if this was the demographic trend for the group. I agitatedly rubbed my temples.

"Shall we begin, people," a man who I assumed was the 'leader' of the secret group announced, clapping his hands like a teacher in an unruly assembly; then again, so far it did seem that it was appropriate, given the visitors so far.

Three of us sat down, spaced as far apart as possible, not just because of the two-metre rule. The rest refused to conform.

"Thank you all for coming. So, this is our first meeting, and I'm quite impressed with the turnout."

I looked around; there was five of us, four of which were

probably still in their late teens, plus the leader. I'd already heard enough. I stood up, scraping the floor to an uncomfortable audible level, causing everyone to turn and look at me. I winced, due to both the noise and the attention equally.

"Ah, fantastic. Hello there, thanks for volunteering to go first. It can always be a bit nerve-racking, but clearly someone of your.... maturity has the confidence needed." He gestured to me, as if to say, 'the floor is all yours'!

Should I be honest and tell them that I was just heading for the door to leave, or the truth about my feelings towards the topic of the group, which was to get to the bottom of *why* we had been in lockdown for so long, *why* progress wasn't being made as it should; what my own personal beliefs in the matter were? I decided on none of those and just briefly introduced myself.

"Hi, my name is Nicole," I started, hoping I wouldn't need to elaborate.

"Hi, Nicole, I'm Keith," the leader replied overenthusiastically.

I swiftly sat down, hoping to avoid further probing. There was a long, awkward pause. The last time I had been in this situation was when I registered with a weight loss group and had to pay a fiver to stand on the scales and be told that I was fat in front of a room full of equally large women.

Of course, back then £5 was worth a lot more than it was now. It would have probably cost more for a packet of biscuits for this meeting. If biscuits were still available.

"Does nobody else want to introduce themselves then?" Keith asked, with a hint of desperation in his voice. Another awkward silence. "Ok, ermmmm, ok, so... ermm... yes, so let's get started. We are here to discuss our theories about why all this is happening to us right now, and then the eventual goal is to find a solution.

"So in March of 2020 we experienced a lockdown caused by a virus that swept across the world, killing over 50,000 people in its first six months. A second lockdown hit most of the world in the November, and we are still in it now. Most people believed that this was 100% fact, but slowly we, as a population, created so many conspiracy theories that nobody really feels like a deadly virus was accidentally released to a whole planet or that one person eating a bat in China caused this.

"There have been theories such as a controlled mass cull of an overpopulated species; either for a rebirth of Earth and all its other species that have been fighting to survive the destruction caused by us humans or simply to protect the world's resources by reducing its inhabitants.

"The introduction of 5G was said to have caused it. Does anyone wish to elaborate this further?" The only noise in the room was uncomfortable shifting of people in chairs, or feet shuffling for those who remained standing. "Ok..... does anyone have any other theories?"

"That myran clock," the juvenile in the red baseball cap blurted out.

"Thank you, ermm, what's your name please?" You could see he pressure lift away from Keith when he spoke.

"Kirk," he replied.

"Excellent, Kirk," Keith smiled, "Can you elaborate?"

"You know, the myran clock that they stopped making."

"It's the repitilians," announced a voice from the back, as she shuffled forward and took a seat.

"The repitilians?" Keith repeated.

"Yeah, all of the 'people'," she used the finger quotes for this, "in power, like prime ministers, royalty and presidents are all repitilians sent here to control us."

"Right...." Keith nodded, the cogs clearly working in his brain to make a connection. "So the 'repitilians' released the virus into the atmosphere to control us further, or maybe to take over the world? Is that what you mean, ermmm...."

"Yeah, they're here to take over the world. They come from a distant planet, not in our solar system. Their planet died and Earth is the only hosipitable planet they could go to. Their whole race is floating in a massive spaceship in space, and once the powerful repitilians have taken over, the others will come down and inhabit the world instead."

"Ok, interesting theory, erm...." he again gestured to the woman to relinquish her name, but she failed to detect it. "So they will live here on our *hospitable* planet once all humans have been killed, or just to an acceptable level until there are more, erm... 'repitilians' as the majority ethnic group, for word of a better phrase?"

"Dunno, maybe that's something we need to discuss at this meeting?"

"I think she means *'Reptilians'*, Keith?" I suggested, instantly regretting it.

"Ah, yes, yes, I see, erm.... definitely, erm...." still no name from Jane Doe. "Ok, any other theories?"

"Aliens," youth number two piped up.

"Ok, erm....." he gestured for a name.

"Travis," he obliged.

"Great, Travis, was this not what, erm...." he pointed at the woman, nodding at her too.

"What's your name?" I broke the silence.

"Oh, it's Donna," she finally responded.

"Thank you, Donna," Keith breathed a sigh of relief, "so is this not the same as the, ermmm.... *Reptilians*?" He gestured to Donna and myself.

"Nah," Travis replied, "these aliens come from a different planet. From, um, um, well I don't know. I don't know the answers to all this."

"Oh, that's not a problem, Travis, that's the reason for this group."

"God," the last 'member' of the group, sat at the other end of the room, added. "He was angry with us for all of the war, so he's killing us all. All the bad people."

"Ok...."

"Nah," Travis interrupted, "my grandad died from the 'Rona, he wasn't a bad person."

"Was he a soldier in a war, though?" member number five responded.

"Nah, he was a engineer."

'AN engineer', I breathed silently. "Oh, Hell!" I said, out loud, I guess.

"Ah!" Keith jumped back into life. "Hell. Now this is interesting!"

"We're in Hell?" Travis gasped.

"O.M.G., no way!" Kirk gasped.

"When?" number five gasped.

When everyone had finished gasping, Keith composed himself. "Ok, when indeed. The virus hit us badly in March, leading to the lockdown."

I was sure he'd already said this. "It was discovered, or created in 2019 though, wasn't it? Hence the name COVID-19?"

"Right, ok. So sometime in 2019 we all died and walked into Hell?" Keith mused.

"When?" number five repeated.

I was known for my problem-solving abilities, especially at Scrabble and Cluedo. "Let's think back to when things started going wrong for us then."

Silence fell upon the group.

"Ok, we, erm.... need a little time to think. Shall we have coffee?" Keith suggested.

We poured our coffees and relocated to different areas of the old village hall, removing our masks. I managed to tolerate a coffee which contained more milk and sugar than the coffee itself. The caffeine and sugar seemed to boost all six of us up. We each replaced our masks and returned to our seats.

"So, back to the start of Hell then?" Keith broke through the buzzing chatter. "Any thoughts?"

"Yes," Donna replied confidently. "In 2016, that year 'from Hell'," she did the finger quote thing again.

"Yes," number five agreed. "All those famous people died."

"My gran died then too," Travis announced.

"My George died then too," Donna explained.

I felt a little tug of my heart strings. "Oh, Travis, Donna, that's so sad."

"It was heart-wrenching for me when I lost George."

"Was he your husband?" I enquired.

"He could have been," she explained, "but circumstances prevented it. I loved him so much." Donna wiped away a small tear.

I turned to Travis, "So was it the gran that lived with your grandad who died from COVID?"

"Did you know her then?" Travis questioned.

I shook my head and looked back at Donna. "Christmas

Day, as well," she continued, as if Travis had never spoken, which was fine by me.

"Ok, so 2016 then? Do we think that, maybe, we entered Hell, say.... New Year's Day 2016 then?"

"It was the year that Trump became president," Donna added, attention diverted from her George fella. "One of the repitilians who controls the world."

"It was the year of Brexit too," number five added.

"All those that voted for Brexit must have been repitilians then," Donna deduced. "They must have taken over parts of Earth to be able to do it then."

"Reptilians just invaded UK at first then, Donna?" I said sarcastically.

She didn't notice the sarcasm. "Well if there were so many famous people dying then I suppose that gave them some room. Obviously the repitilians started their mass take-over in 2020 when 'COVID' arrived."

"So do we think that the repitilians, sorry Reptilians," Keith gestured to me, "voted for Brexit or forced people to vote for it?"

"Both is possible, I guess, but I think it was them. They've been taking over for years, the queen is a repitilian, and all her family, so it goes back a long time, but it's the repitilian's decisions that are causing us to end up in Hell."

"Interesting," Keith said.

"Since 2013, there have been more deaths in the world

due to natural disasters than war," Kirk announced, reading from him mobile phone.

"Wow, what a statistic, Kirk, thanks," Keith replied.

"So the repitilians have killed all these people to make room for them."

"But... surely if all of these millions of deaths happen, who are the Reptilians taking over? Wouldn't an official lower death rate mean that Reptilians could replace the unofficial ones so nobody noticed?" I couldn't believe that I was actually discussing Reptilians with these people. "And wouldn't it just be that we were on Earth still, rather than Hell?"

"All those who have died since 2012 are in Heaven, like Travis' gran and grandad, and Donna's George, and we are in Hell, then the repitilians are on Earth," Kirk stated.

"So where's the Devil then?" number five interjected.

"Where's God?" I retorted. "'God' is in 'Heaven' as much as 'Satan' is in Hell. Just by living, or not living, in a place, doesn't mean that the deity has to be visible and present." I had found myself using finger quotes and releasing my inner atheist.

"But it doesn't seem hot, like Hell," number five stated.

"That's just what an image that God-fearing people created, to cause conformity," I explained.

"Huh?" number five replied.

"Your George, Donna," Travis interjected, "It's George Michael, innit? He died on Christmas Day on 2016."

Donna nodded. "Yes, he was my world."

"So if it started in 2012 then, it was the myran clock then?"

"Do you mean the Mayan calendar, Kirk?" I sighed.

<u>QUEEN CORONA LIVES!!</u>

How are you feeling?

A little wheezy maybe?

A bit of a temperature?

Confused? How confused?

How many stories are there in this book?

Are you sure? 'Nineteen' certainly wasn't the nineteenth story in the collection.

In fact, there a lot of numbers within this book of short stories. 'Three's Company' – shouldn't that be 'Two's Company'? and 'Four's a Crowd'??

I like confusion.

I like people being unhappy.

In pain.

Sick.

I'm sure every time you get a symptom, you'll worry that you have the virus. And I like that, I like that a lot!!

Five G? What's that all about? More numbers to confuse you all, maybe? How can an improvement of a wireless network cause a pandemic, if indeed a pandemic is what it is!

Was it a natural virus, or borne in a laboratory?

Who, or what, created me?

Was it a god-fearing community?

Aliens?

A creature in the night?

Was it intentional, or an accident?

A man eating a bat? Or indeed a bat devouring a man?

There are people out there who think we are now in Hell, does that make me the Devil? Don't worry, that doesn't bother me. It's all a case of mind over matter; I don't mind and you don't matter!

I am Queen Corona! I am going to ensure that everyone suffers, because of me, at some point in their life! Whether there are no more holidays, or fights over toilet roll!

Some of these stories are true, some most definitely are not!

......

....

....

....

What are you looking for? An answer? Oh, my dears, I'm not going to TELL you. That would be far too simple! I so enjoy watching you blame each other!

ABOUT THE AUTHOR

Lisa is married to Rich, has 3 children, 1 granddaughter
(with a second on the way!) and many cats.
Born and bred in Leicester, she lived in Kent for 10 years
and now resides in Derby.

Other books by Lisa J Rivers:
Why I have So Many Cats (poetry)
Winding Down (novel)
Searching (Follow-up to Winding Down)

For details of our other books, or for information about submitting your manuscript please visit our website

www.green-cat.co

GREEN CAT BOOKS

Made in the USA
Coppell, TX
04 June 2021

56871817R00115